ALPINE GLOW

ROBIN BALOGH COX

KNOWHERE MEDIA

©2015

DISCLAIMER

The characters and events portrayed in this book are fictitious. Any similarity to real persons, living or dead, is coincidental and not intended by the author.

This book is intended for entertainment purposes only. The author and publisher, Knowhere Media LLC, shall have neither liability nor responsibility to any person or entity with respect to any loss or damage caused, or alleged to have been caused, directly or indirectly, by the information contained in this book.

I would like to dedicate this book to my two beautiful sisters, Darci and Terri, true artists without whom I would not have been inspired to attempt writing my stories. They have been my encouragement, my editors and my motivation not only in my writing, but in my life. Thank you!

1

Bev carefully navigated the turning ribbon of road through the last of the high desert outcroppings. The golden morning light was turning white across the open plains ahead. The road sign read: Alpine 10 Miles.

"Crap."

She hadn't anticipated how long the twenty-mile drive from Fort Davis would take. She was late.

Fumbling through her bag, she blindly found the print out she had made at the hotel. She absently sped up on the open stretch of road and read the directions on the dash in front of her. A hand full of hearty cows and a few antelope grazed on the open grassy fields ignoring her as she whizzed by.

The job interview was at 10am, it was 9:57, better call. Fumbling again she found her cell phone. It beeped at her nonchalantly when she opened it. No service, perfect, bad first impression.

The job was only part-time, maybe there wouldn't be too many applicants. Heck look around, she was the only soul as far as she could see in this part of south Texas. The grassland plains spread for miles, nothing but the smoky mountaintops of Mexico far away in the distance and a few puffy white clouds desperately hanging on the horizon.

The black and white Mustang seemed to materialize from out of nowhere, lights flashing behind her.

"Well, hell," she muttered and reluctantly slowed, pulling off on the narrow shoulder.

She watched the big, barrel chested officer approach, clipboard in hand. It was a wonder he could cram himself into the small speedy version of a cop car. He was obviously proud of his occupation. His uniform was impeccable, if not a bit tight, his glasses were mirrored, the beige Stetson was brushed. He touched the front brim as he came to the window.

"Ma'am?" The moniker demanded an answer without any further question.

"I'm sorry officer, I'm late for an interview and I wasn't paying attention."

"No need for apologies. License and registration please," he spoke a bit too slowly she thought, deliberately delaying the interchange. She fumbled in her bag once more and produced the documents.

"What exactly are you pulling me over for?" She asked. He ignored the question and glanced at the license.

"Beverly Connors. Is this address current?" She could see herself in his glasses, she was pinching her forehead together in an expression that made her look like her mother.

"Gad," she thought. "No, I just moved from Denver. I'm staying at a hotel in Fort Davis. Just trying to be a good citizen and get a job."

As soon as she said it she was sorry. The sarcasm wasn't lost on him, one eyebrow raised over his glasses.

"Sit tight Miss Connors, I'll just run this through the computer," he smiled mechanically and walked slowly back to his car.

She would never get there. It was the only job in the classified section of the tiny paper that had even remotely interested her.

Wanted, Freelance Writer for the Alpine Avalanche
Part time. Paid by the story.

She glanced in the mirror. Officer Macho was still in the driver's seat, he seemed to fill the cab. "I can't believe they can fit a computer in there," she thought to herself. "Was he taking a drink of coffee!?" She dropped her shoulders, took a deep breath and gave in.

Her situation wasn't all bad. The air was still cool and smelled sweet coming over the grasses into her open window. That was one of the unexpected pleasures she had discovered coming to this part of the country. How cool the nights were. It reminded her of home. It was one of the reasons she had decided to stay. Or try to. Without work she would have to keep moving. Finally, there was movement behind her.

"Miss Connors," he handed back her papers with one more. "I'm citing you for exceeding the speed limit. You were going 79 in a 60."

"Oh, come on! I just told you I'm new in town, a tourist! I had no idea!"

He ignored her pleas, "You will have to contact the courthouse in Fort Davis to pay your fine within two weeks. It's written on the back along with the phone number." He slowly removed his glasses and leaned on the roof of the car. For the first time she could see his eyes, grey, long lashed and set slightly close together. If she didn't know better she'd say they were twinkling. He was actually enjoying this cat and mouse game!

She leveled her gaze to his, "I believe I will appeal this, Officer...?" She looked frantically for his name on the ticket and then his badge.

"Gant," he responded, pulling his name badge out from his shirt for her to see. "Samuel Gant, Miss Connors."

"It's *Mrs*," she retorted, "and I am extremely late, will there be anything else?" Her hands were gripping the wheel causing her knuckles to turn white.

"No, Ma'am." He straightened and replaced his sunglasses, "Just slow down...Mrs. Connors."

She pulled back onto the road. Of all the nerve. Slow down. She purposely floored the accelerator until she reached 60. It seemed as if she was crawling. Now she desperately needed the job that she hadn't even interviewed for. How much were speeding tickets in the middle of nowhere? What a racket. Her ranting brought her to the edge of town.

SHE BURST through the door of the Alpine paper at 10:38, front door bell jangled. She had missed the building once and had to park down the street a few blocks. She tried to regain her composure as she waited in the lobby for the receptionist to return.

The room was sparse, a metal desk, two plastic and chrome chairs against the opposite wall, a dying plant in the window. It smelled like dust and newsprint. No one came. She peered down the hall to the left, small offices also empty.

"Hello?" No answer. "Hello?" She said louder. No one.

She glanced at her watch, 10:45. No doubt the interviewer had long given up on her showing. Were those voices she heard? She followed the sound to the right. Voices and machinery. They obviously printed the paper here. There were double doors at the end of the hall with windows. She could see the work room and people moving intentionally around the machinery. Perhaps someone in there would know where she should go.

The noise was ten times louder when she stepped through the doors. The press shook the floor in waves. Huge rolls of paper were sifting through at amazing speeds. A Hispanic man in grey work clothes had his back to her.

"Excuse me," she yelled, or thought she yelled. He didn't respond. "Excuse me!!" She screamed and touched his shoulder. He jumped causing her to jump. "Sorry," she mouthed, shrugging her shoulders.

He placed his hand over his heart and staggered back in a mock heart attack and grinned, revealing a set of the most stunning white teeth she had ever seen. He indicated the door and they both went back into the hall.

"You scared me lady! What can I do for you?" He pulled orange ear plugs from his head.

"Sorry, I'm late for an interview with a..." She glanced at the paper, "Mr. Preston. Do you know where I can find him?"

He checked the clock through the doors of the workroom, "He goes to the police station at 11:00, probably went to the bank or post office first."

"Should I wait?" She asked looking around vaguely.

"If you want, but he usually doesn't get back until after lunch. One-ish." It was his turn to shrug. Again he grinned. This time the charm was gone.

"Maybe I'll try to catch him at the police station. Which way would that be?"

"Two blocks down, on the right."

He replaced the earplugs and entered the double doors, a burst of sound escaped as he disappeared.

"Great," she paused outside for a moment. The car was to the left, the police station to the right. The air was no longer cool. In fact, the sun was sharp on her forehead. It beat down on the concrete walk, bouncing back up her leg. It was shady to the right.

"What the hell," she said as she turned right.

The police station was better staffed. There were two women at the front desk wearing police uniforms, which were not doing either one of them any fashion favors.

"Women working in a man's world that gives no concessions for the female frame," Bev thought.

The younger woman was very pale, her dark hair cut in a bob that made her round face look rounder and her skin lighter. The older woman's hair was teased in a high pile and she wore what appeared to be theatrical make up and acrylic nails that clicked the keyboard on which she was intently typing.

"Excuse me," Bev leaned casually on the raised counter hoping to find some camaraderie. The young woman stared, the older kept typing.

"What can we help you with, Hon?" Her nails continued...*click, click, click.*

"I'm trying to find Mr. Preston from the paper. One of the pressmen told me he might be here."

"Are you a reporter?" *Click, click, click.*

"Oh, no. I mean, well, I would like to be. I was meeting him for a job interview."

The clicking stopped and both women now stared

seeming to size her up. Perhaps they recognized one of their own kind, a woman, trying to do a traditionally masculine job. The clicking continued. Perhaps not.

"Second door on the right, down that hall," she indicated the direction with the nod of her beehive head. The young receptionist slowly followed her with a hauntingly empty gaze.

She could see that there were three men in the small office ahead of her. The officer behind the desk was leaning back on his chair, hands raised over his balding head, his belly pushing the limits of his uniform and nearly touching the edge of his desk. In one hand he held his hat and with the other he scratched what red hair he had left. His expression was concerned, maybe even baffled.

The other gentleman in sight sat on the opposite side of the desk with his back to the open door. He was obviously tall, gauging from his long neck and the way he had to fold his legs to cross them in front of the desk. He was a sharp contrast to the heavy officer with his thick long hair and hallow frame. The third man was another policeman, judging from the pant leg and the boot that was visible.

She could hear bits of the conversation before she reached the door.

"I don't care, Mac! We can't keep this from everybody. It's newsworthy! You know how hard it is to fill that paper. This is actually interesting and you're telling me to keep a lid on it." The tall man un-tangled his legs and put both hands on the desk, they were long and lean too.

"I didn't say you could never print it, Hal. I'm just asking you to keep it quiet until we're sure what we're dealing with. I don't want a panic on my hands." For as soft as the officer looked he had a steely voice that demanded obedience. The tall man relaxed and sat back.

"For now," Hal Preston conceded. Bev cleared her throat and knocked on the door frame.

"Excuse me," she said for what seemed like the eightieth time that day. All eyes turned, chairs straightened.

"Yes, Ma'am. What can I do for you?" Officer "Mac" asked.

"I am looking for Mr. Preston. I'm Beverly Connors. I have, I mean, *had* an interview with him earlier."

Hal Preston clamored, stood to his full height and extended his hand. She was right, he was at least 6'4".

"I'm Hal Preston. I'm glad you caught up with me Miss Connors. This is Officer Matt McNeely, we call him Mac. The big man rose half way and shook her hand as well.

"Nice to meet you," Mac's handshake was sure and confident.

"Still formidable," she thought.

"I read your resume this morning. Impressive. Are you sure we can entertain you enough with our humble mountain paper? Miss Connors has a Masters in Journalism from DU," Hal offered.

She glanced around the room. Slightly unnerved by the group interview.

"I'm looking for something part time right now, nothing grandiose," she regretted using the word, it sounded showy. She began to sweat, "Something not so fast paced." She tried to recover, "I came out here to, oh I don't know, to..."

"Slow down?" It was the first time she had really looked at the officer in the corner. He stood and reached out his hand.

"Officer Sam Gant. Miss Connors."

She hadn't recognized him without his hat and glasses. He grinned warmly this time, that same playful look in his grey eyes.

"*Mrs.* Connors," she corrected, completely befuddled. "I give up," she thought and took his hand.

"When can you start, Mrs. Connors?" Hal interjected.

"Tomorrow?" Bev was momentarily confused. Had she just gotten the job?

"Great, I will fill you in tomorrow morning at the paper, say at nine? I'm glad you and Gant have met. You'll be working very closely with him on the police reports." Hal made his way past her through the door.

"Oh." She glanced at Officer Gant, he was still grinning. "Nine?" She verified.

"Yes, nine. Try not to be late Mrs. Connors. Papers are dated material. Important to be on time," and Hal was gone in three long steps.

"Look forward to working with you Mrs. Connors." Officer Gant emphasized "Mrs." as he donned his official disguise and also slipped past her. She was left standing in the doorway.

"I got the job," she said to no one in particular.

"Looks like it," Mac had an "is there anything else" look on his face.

"Thanks," Bev said weakly and bowed out of his office and out of the police station into the noonday heat.

2

Jacob Lauren Murray, leaned casually on the horn of his saddle spitting over the shoulder of the bay beneath him. The saddle leather creaked, even under his wiry frame. His horse shifted to his other hip adjusting to his rider. The shade that the mesquite bush had provided earlier was quickly evaporating in the late morning sun. Jake began to question his father's plan. Why would they try during the day? The water could easily be found any moonlit night, especially by thirsty cattle. He and the bay took a deep breath nearly in unison. He patted the pony's neck.

"Just a little longer and we'll head back," Jake promised the horse.

The only indication that the horse was awake was the twitch of his ears as he listened to his rider. The locust buzzed in turn down the ravine, taking short arcing flights to the next tuft of bear grass. The heat brought the scent of salt cedar and grease wood up the canyon on a slight breeze that was far from refreshing. In an hour the canyon would be blazing with direct noonday heat. Even the birds were settling in for siestas this time of day. Jake took off his hat and mopped his forehead with a rag from his front pocket.

"Shit." The explicative covered a gamut of emotions. He replaced the hat and rag and squinted down the canyon.

The Caversons had been stealing water for weeks, maybe months. Bringing their cattle in through this canyon and stopping on the edge of the Murray's land, using the Murray's watering hole. Fences had been torn down and the Murray's own cattle had to be rounded up, they had lost a couple dozen head. It had to be stopped. Caversons could drive their cattle through conventional trails and pay the per head fee at the conventional watering holes. Jacob's father, Lionel Murray, was determined to stop them. But first they had to catch them.

Jake and his brother Clint had taken turns at this post above the canyon in hopes of catching the thieves red handed. So far, a week's worth of watching and no sign of any of them or their blasted cows. There were so many other things Jake would rather be doing. Drinking, screwing, even mending fence, or castrating steers would be better than this! He spit again.

Suddenly his horse lifted his head and cocked his ears forward, looking down the canyon.

Jake, with the instinct of a horseman followed the animal's gaze, taking advantage of the enhanced sight, hearing and smell the horse allowed. Both he and the horse stiffened and waited. A distant echo first, clattering hoof on rock and then the distinct low of moving cattle came up the canyon long before the herd was visible. Jake's heart beat heavily and the horse's nostrils flared at the new scent and sound coming toward them. Soon the lead animal, a Longhorn, pushed around the bend followed by about thirty head and three riders.

"Shit," Jake muttered again. This time in disbelief and disappointment.

Now the Murrays would actually have to do something. He couldn't identify the riders yet but the cattle weren't his, he knew that much.

They drove the animals slowly like seasoned cattlemen. Moving cows too fast in this heat would lead to exhaustion. Still the animals could smell water and they began to get anxious. Lowing became bellowing and the cowboys worked hard to keep them from breaking out into a trot. Clouds of dust were being kicked up.

"One shot," thought Jake, and he slowly reached for his six-shooter on his hip.

His horse quivered. Jake's plan was quickly squelched by his father's words of warning before he left.

"Don't do anything rash, boy!" The old man had bellowed at him. "Just make sure it's them. We'll take care of it together."

Why did it always have to be a family affair? Jake could pop off all three of them before they knew the first one dropped. The cattle would scatter, no one would be the wiser.

"You hear me boy!?" Lionel Murray's voice rung in Jacob's head.

He obediently let go of the butt of the gun. The cattle and riders where right in front of them now. Jake watched them in silence, sweat pouring down his back and down his face. He dare not move to the shade now. His horse was sweating too, itching to jump into the fray. Jake could see the rider's faces, ruddy with heat and determination. It was definitely the Caversons, the two younger brothers, Jace and Carson, and their older cousin Marshall. Old Man Caverson and his oldest son Seth were nowhere to be seen.

The three men whistled and moved on their mounts still keeping the cattle at a slow trot. As fast as they came, they passed, and Jake watched the dust settle behind them as they moved up the canyon. The small herd plunged headlong into the only water source for miles. A slow burn began in his belly. That was his water, his family's water. When he was certain he was beyond their detection, he reined his horse quickly around and headed back to the ranch house. His father would be proud of his discretion.

THE MURRAY RANCH sprawled over 12,000 dry, yucca and scrub brush covered acres of the southern Texas territory, about twenty square miles. The cattle that could survive out here were thin and tough skinned. Usually a Longhorn-Brahma cross that were easy to breed, calve and sell to the Mexican meat markets. There was little money in it, the land alone was where the family got their prosperity and only land with water was worthy. The more acres you owned in this part of the world the more your family was respected by the gun toting government that ruled the west and the greater chance of finding water.

Land, and the water rights that came with it, changed hands in the most nefarious ways; gambling, theft, and even murder, were just a few. They went to deserving brothers by brothers not so deserving and vice versa.

The Murray family were only the second generation land owners. Earl Lawson Murray had purchased the first 10,000 acres after the territories independence from Mexico in 1836. The last 2800 acres had been fought for by the Murrays over the last generation in skirmishes with the Mexican government and various Mexican border dwellers.

The land had claimed the lives of the entire first generation of Murrays to occupy it through disease, drought, and dust choking work. It had claimed three of this generation's sons through bloodshed and violence.

Either way the price seemed too high to Jacob. Disputes over barren land, bitter water, and boney cows seemed senseless to him. But, he was a Murray.

His bay pulled up fast to the hitching post outside the main house. Dust flying around his legs, Jacob barely let the horse stop before sliding off and bounding up the front porch. The temperature dropped noticeably even in the thin shade under the eaves. Lunch had already been served. The hired men would be napping on the east side of the buildings trying to rest during the heat of the day. Lionel Murray always took this time to stretch out on the floor of the ranch house office at the back of the house.

"Pa?" Jacob could see his boot bottoms as he turned the corner.

"Mm-hmm," the elder Murray had been asleep. "Did you see um, Jake?" He asked.

"Yeah, it was them," Jake made himself slow and leaned against the door frame, "Three youngest Caverson boys and about 30 head."

"Mm-hmm," Lionel Murray was no longer sleepy, Jacob could almost hear his mind clicking. "Call your brother, we need to set this right."

Jacob, sighed and squinted into the dark room to better see his father's face staring up at the ceiling. He was suddenly hotter, more tired and hungrier than he remembered. He wanted to baulk at the instruction, make an excuse. He paused too long.

"Go, Jake!" The old man barked and Jake, as usual, jumped to his bidding.

3

It was 8:45. She had made it and had even obeyed the speed limits, cussing Sam Gant under her breath the whole way. She was just about to walk through the front door of the paper when she spotted Hal Preston striding down the sidewalk carrying three cups of coffee. She paused and waited to hold the door for her new boss.

"Good morning! Very prompt! Thanks!" He handed her an insulated cup.

"This is Elena," he indicated the young Hispanic woman behind the metal desk.

"Ahhh, the mysterious disappearing receptionist," Bev thought to herself. Hal handed her one of the remaining cups.

"Elena, Beverly Connors, a new writer."

Elena, dipped her head slightly and sat down with her cup.

"Good morning," Bev said to both of them.

"Come on back," Hal turned down the left hall that had been empty on her visit the day before and entered the last office on the left.

It took her several more steps than he to cover the same distance. It struck Bev that he looked and moved like a crane. Even his face had crane-like qualities, bright eyes, long hooked beak, as if ready to pounce on the next bite of information.

"Have a seat," he indicated one of the dated institutional office chairs opposite his desk.

She unloaded her computer bag and purse from her shoulder and settled down with her coffee. His office was functional, no personal items. On the table against the far wall was a chaotic pile of newspapers from around the world and clippings of major news events. They were the only indication of what she imagined was the hectic pace of the lone newspaper man.

"I'm sorry I had to be so hasty yesterday. Wednesday is press day. The paper goes out at midnight. There are always lots of last minute edits and fires to put out. Sometimes literally," he chuckled and she grinned, not knowing exactly what he meant but imagining the mechanical difficulties of the huge machine she had witness rocking the press room floor the day before.

"No problem. I understand. I must admit it was the shortest job interview I have ever had. Where I got the job at least." She took a sip of the coffee allowing him to continue.

"Let me tell you the details of the job and you can decide if you still want to take it. It's part time and paid by the story like the ad said. I can pay $250 per story unless it's a barn burner, then it's $500. I alone can decide if it's printable and what it's worth. Most of your leads will be given to you but I am open to suggestions for topics. I especially want you to check on the police reports daily, follow up any interesting stories," he paused to take a sip from his cup

"Officer Gant," she said flatly.

"Mm. Good man, knows this town and the people. He will be an invaluable resource for you." He tapped the side of his cup with his long finger.

"Invaluable." She saw those grey glinting eyes.

"What do you think?" Hal Preston cocked his head slightly making him look even more crane-like.

She paused slightly longer than he expected and his face began to fall into worry.

"Great! Yes!" She hastily accepted.

Bev did the math quickly in her head. She could do one or two stories a week and make ends meet for now. She wondered how many "barn burner" stories were available in Alpine.

"Good! Good! I could use some journalistic company! You can have an office here if you'd like. Copy for review needs to be on my desk by noon on Tuesday. Here are some leads from last week that didn't get covered and you can check in with Gant daily for more. Ask Elena if you need any supplies. Looking forward to seeing some of your work," Hal stood handing her a file folder, indicating the meeting was over.

"Thanks, I'll do my best."

She left him to his clippings.

There were four other offices with the same grey metal furniture in them, all uninhabited. She chose the second one down on the right, far enough away from the boss to have privacy but close enough to hear him if he called.

She carefully set up her lap top and checked her e-mail. At least there was an internet connection. She would have to get a longer range plan for the cell phone. Apparently "nationwide" coverage didn't include this lost little part of the world.

She took another sip of coffee and opened the file folder.

There were a few clippings from area papers. One about a car dealer in Fort Stockton that had been ripping people off looked promising. There were also several official print outs from the national park service and the local police. Nothing on these jumped out at her.

She asked Elena about using a land line phone and made a couple of calls to Fort Stockton. The dealer wouldn't comment and she could only find one disgruntled elderly woman from the list of supposed victims. The woman's grievances could have filled a whole column but they all seemed rather petty and Bev wasn't sure if she wasn't making them up just to have someone to talk to. She tried in vain to rewrite some of the existing copy from the article for a lead into some new material but was quickly stumped. Great. Three hours spent on a dead end.

She dreaded the thought of her next move. She would have to go to Gant. On the other hand, why give in so soon. After all she had nearly a week to find a story and she really didn't want to give him the satisfaction. Maybe she could scout out a story for herself.

She packed up, asked Elena about lunch spots, and headed out into her new territory.

Alpine Texas: Elevation 4,481 feet, population approximated 6500. Established in 1888 by virtue of available water, it became a railroad stop on the east west Southern Pacific line and a cattle trail crossing from Mexico to the northern plains of the Texas panhandle. The vast open Chihuahuan desert that surrounded it had been home to pioneers, Indians, Mexican and American armies, then ranchers and immigrants, and finally a unique breed of mountain desert dwellers including homeland security professionals, retirees and hippies.

The town retained its youth through the accredited Sul Ross University which towered over the town on the northeast. The night life was lively. Book rooms, music festivals and art galleries kept things current and cultural. Considered a "border" town, even though the border with Mexico to the south was nearly 100 miles away. Mexican Folk Art flavor, people and contraband seeped over the border and were found in everything from the food to the architecture to the residents of the local jail.

The town location, tucked into an ancient volcanic valley, heats the streets in the summer but also keeps the temperatures mild in the winter. And then there are those cool desert nights, and the billions of stars that are visible on the moonless nights. A person could get lost here and easily forget the past, "Out Where the West Begins," as the sign says at the edge of town.

Getting lost seemed to be Bev's specialty lately. How could navigating this tiny town be so difficult? Maybe it was the 360 degrees of foothills and mountains that was throwing her off. She had made at least a dozen U-turns today. It was easier with the Rockies, in Denver they were always to the west.

"If you get lost just head towards the mountains, that's west," her Dad had instructed her when she first started venturing off on her own in the city.

Despite his best intentions there were many nights when the mountains weren't in view and Bev and her gaggle of girlfriends would be lost as geese. A wave of sadness came over her. So much had changed this last year. A car horn shook her out of her personal fog, the light had turned.

She had spent the better part of the last two days researching Alpine and trying to get her bearings. She had found the drive in burger joint, the gas station with the best price and the small college library. That was all she needed for now.

The archive library at the college had endless information but it was the people that really impressed Bev. Worn, sepia photos of solemn faces, braving the harsh west for fortunes in cattle, gold and land. And the women, so covered, so young but showing age beyond their years in their faces and eyes. She was sure she didn't have the "right stuff" to be a rancher's wife or a pioneer back then. She could barely take care of herself in the 21st century. The cell phone situation was getting serious. Without it she felt lost, pathetic.

She unpacked her computer at the now familiar table near the library reading room. She was thinking that maybe a historical piece about the fire of 1881 might be her first offering to Hal Preston. She knew in the back of her mind that she was deliberately avoiding any contact with Officer Gant, but she ignored the thought and absorbed herself in the work at hand.

SHE WAS SPINNING, spinning, faster and faster. The night sky looked like a blender of stars going round and round and the snowflakes spun dizzyingly out of control. Occasionally they hit her face and stung in the icy wind. She laughed, but it sounded so far away, tinny and thin in the crisp mountain air. Music piped over the speakers, unidentifiable. Suddenly with a thud the spinning stopped, her head however continued to whirl but other than her pride she was unhurt.

"Bev?, Beverly? Are you all right?" Her father's concerned face came into view as he moved across the ice. "Get up Beverly, you'll get cold." She started to protest. "Beverly, get up."

"In a minute," she said. Her father laughed and held out his hand.

"Beverly, it's closing time, get up."

Her father's voice changed to a hushed urgent whisper.

"Beverly. Miss Connors?"

Suddenly the mountain night faded into the harsh institutional light of the Alpine Library.

With a start, Beverly jumped. A large man was gently shaking her shoulder.

"Beverly, it's me, Sam Gant, Officer Gant." His gaze was curious. Bev focused, seeing him for the first time.

"Oh, Officer," she said, still bleary eyed. "I guess I dozed off."

"Yeah, dozed off." He smiled, she immediately came to her senses.

"What time is it?" She nervously wiped the drool off her chin, how long had she been out?

"Midnight, closing time." He was watching her with an amused expression on his face.

"Oh, sorry." She scrambled to put her papers and laptop in various carrying bags. Why did this guy unnerve her so badly?

"No hurry, I have the keys. I sent Anne home." He shook them then he paused, "Must have been some dream."

"It's those eyes, those damn twinkling eyes," she thought again.

"Dream? Why do you say that?" She continued to pack, trying to look busy. Her wall was back up.

"Well, you had a smile on your face," he smirked, "thinking of anyone in particular?"

"Excuse me?" If the tone didn't shoot him down the daggers in her eyes as she turned to face him would.

"I'm just saying that you looked..." he shrugged, "happy."

"Officer Gant, I don't believe you know me well enough to tell when I'm happy."

She had managed to gather her belongings and move purposefully towards the door. He followed, turning lights off behind them.

"I beg to differ." He was undeterred by the chill in her tone, "I think I can tell when a woman is happy."

"Oh, you can?" It was her turn to smile. "Well you would be the first, Officer Gant!"

They stopped at the front glass doors together. He chuckled easily, no offense taken.

"Allow me to escort you to your car ma'am." His tone was official.

"Thank you officer." So was hers.

"SHIT." The car made a wheezing attempt at turning over. She tried again. *Click, click.* Nothing.

"Ohhhhh!" The sound was part pain, part exhaustion, part exasperation. The patrol car pulled back in beside her where it had just pulled out.

Gant rolled down the passenger window and leaned across the front seat. "Won't start?"

"No," she said weakly. Would she never be away from this chivalrous cop?

"Battery?"

She nodded.

"Hop in, I'll take you home."

He popped the door lock.

"Perfect," she muttered to herself. She stuffed all her belongings and herself into half of the bucket seat left on the passenger side, trying not to bump something official.

"I swear I didn't leave the lights on," she thought out loud, apologizing.

"No problem. I am, after all, a servant of the people."

He busied himself driving and she organized the mess at her feet. Soon they were headed out of town on the lonely stretch of highway where their lives had first intersected.

"How's the research coming?" He asked casually as they hummed along in the tripped out sports car. He fit better in the seat than she imagined, like part of the machinery.

"Good, I think." She watched the yellow lines appear out of the pitch black and disappear under the hood instead of looking at him. "It's more interesting than I made it seem tonight, falling asleep and all. I'm looking at some historical pieces. The people in this part of the country are amazingly resilient."

"Mmm. What's the story?" He glanced occasionally at her, making her heart rate increase.

"God, I am pathetic," she rolled her eyes at herself.

"Water rights in the late 1800's. Evidently they caused some discord among ranchers who took the law into their own hands. True western grit stuff." She hoped she sounded professional.

"The Cattleman's Revenge. The fire of 1881?"

Her mouth almost fell open. "Great, a historian too," she thought. The words "invaluable source" kept ringing through her ears. Apparently there would be no way to get around working with Sam Gant.

"Yes, you've heard..." her question was interrupted by sharp static and a voice over the radio.

"Dispatch to Car 91."

Sam Gant turned his full attention to the radio.

"This is Gant, go ahead."

The radio cracked again.

"We have a 904 in progress at 1321 East First Street, fire is in route."

His brow furrowed.

"Headed that way, over." He turned to Bev. "Hold on, we have to go back."

The car spun 180 degrees on a dime. Bev struggled to keep from slamming into the passenger door and out into the prairie and then back into the computer on the center console.

"What's a 904?" She was finally able to ask.

"Fire." The engine whined as the odometer reached 90. "Main Street, one of the empty store fronts." There was no air of sarcasm or chauvinism now. Officer Gant was on full professional alert.

Alpine street lights came into view in moments, and there on the horizon above the main street roof lines was the distinctive orange glow of a large structure fire. Bev's journalistic instinct began to tingle, she could literally smell her first "barn burner".

4

Caverson's property was a night's ride east of the Murray ranch. Clint, Jake and Lionel Murray rode in silence staying in the ravines when possible for better cover. The moon was bright and full and looked near enough to touch. Only an occasional coyote or an owl changed the scenery. They rested as they rode and saved their energy for the morning's confrontation, for which they were all heavily armed.

The plan was to talk first, make their demands, and if Caversons back talked, on Clint's signal, they would shoot to kill. Murray's would be outnumbered but the Caversons wouldn't suspect violence from just three of them. Hopefully they would catch them at breakfast, sleepy eyed, or better yet with their pants down.

Jake's heart still wasn't in it. He'd killed men before, both brown and white, for good and bad reasons, but winning the water rights, protecting the ranch, keeping the legacy alive and all that crap was just that, crap. He had bigger dreams, better ideas, slicker ways of making a buck and a hell of a lot better ways to spend them.

He glanced at his brother, who slept with his head on his chest, eyes covered by his hat. His horse seemed to move lightly on the trail, somehow sensing his rider's need for an even step. Clint loved this land, loved the ranch and the legacy it represented, for the life of him, Jake didn't know why.

They had always been different. Jake was small and wiry, having to scrap for every inch of respect from friend or foe. Clint was tall, and swarthy. He fit the land like an old leather glove, and everyone loved him, especially their father. Jake always had to vie for the attention of the old man, often doing the wrong thing just to get the beating and be noticed. He had long resented Clint, but as they had become men he accepted his role as the lesser son, lifting the blame from his brother and putting it squarely on Lionel Murray. Jake was resigned to do his father's bidding and live in his brother's shadow for now. After all, every man dies, one way or another. One day, Jake's life would be his own.

The Caverson's ranch gate stood stark in the dawning light, the riders picked up their pace. Corrals lined the drive, some with cows and calves some with wild horses. The ranch was stirring with its morning rituals. In the distance, a rooster crowed. With a casual nod Lionel Murray directed his sons to spread out at his flanks, he would begin the meeting and if necessary his sharp shooting sons would finish it.

As suspected the ranch staff were at breakfast in front of the bunkhouse, more disgruntled than startled at the intrusion of their meal. The foreman and two of the dozen laborers came forward at the same time the front door of the main house opened and the two youngest Caverson boys stepped onto the wide grey porch.

Jake and Clint did a quick count to themselves. Thirteen

laborers and five Caversons, three still indoors. Jake watched the door and windows, casing the house, if they tried to shoot from inside he would be able to see them. None of the ranch hands would be out to chores yet, no one would pass up a meal, Jake could smell the biscuits from here, he wouldn't walk away from that either.

The rest of the Caverson clan filed onto the porch, still only in suspenders and breeches. Jake snorted inwardly, "pants down".

"Well, good morning Lionel." Calvin Caverson pulled on his shirt and his suspenders, "To what do we owe the privilege?" His smile was counterfeit, steel eyes faking a welcome.

"Forget the pleasantries, Caverson, you know why we're here," Clint's tone was stern but not really threatening – yet.

"You're going to have to help me out with a little more than that, Clint," he chuckled.

Jake noticed the ranch hands quietly stand and position themselves based on his tone.

"We've been watching you and your boys push cattle through the south trail on our land, you've broke through fence. We've lost a dozen head and you're stealing our water. We want it stopped. We want payment on the cattle."

The list was matter of fact, Lionel Murray had given his demands. Clint and Jake readied for the response.

Cal continued to grin, he was the only one. His boys and his nephew stood by him, stern, half naked and hungry. For a moment Jake pitied them, they didn't really want to be here either. Cal stroked his unshaven silver stubble.

"Well, that is serious," he finally managed. His false smile faded to fictitious concern, he kept his position on the porch. Clint and Jake watched everyone's hands carefully. If they were armed they hid it well. "I take offense to your accusation, but you have caught me at a slight disadvantage, unprepared to defend my honor," he indicated their state of undress.

"Your honor is bullshit. My brother has seen your boys driving your brand and watering on our land. We want payment for the lost cattle and if we see you again, we'll kill you, got it?" Clint's tone was even but definitely threatening this time. Jake waited for the signal.

Cal's friendly façade finally dropped. There would be no apologies, no negotiating, and no whining for a friendly outcome.

"Well, Lionel, then I guess, I'll just have to –"

There was a glint of steel in the morning sunlight. At the same time from the corner of his eye, Jake saw Clint touch the brim of his hat.

Jake moved without feeling, out of complete instinctive control and with a cool even temper. He could hear his heart and breathing in his head, he used his legs to move his horse exactly where he wanted. The ranch hand fell dead before he could level his pistol and the rest of the men could scatter. Gunfire broke mainly from the Murrays, Lionel in front took out two more Mexicans that lunged for his horse. The Caversons jumped in all directions, off, under, and back into the house. Jake was certain he had hit Marshall. Clint headed around the back of the house. Jake and Lionel moved to the nearest cover behind the bunkhouse, unloading a shower of bullets on the fleeing help until they were well out of sight. They wouldn't return, they didn't get paid enough to die, no matter how good the biscuits. Jacob leaned down as he went past the table and stuffed two in his vest pocket.

Clint was shooting from the back of the house, Jake recognized the resound of his six- shooters. A woman screamed in the house. Too bad. Jake liked women, hated to see them get caught in man's business. No one moved in the front or two visible sides of the house. Lionel Murray balanced his rifle butt on his right thigh, his six-shooter in his left hand.

"Ready?" The question was also a command.

"Mm," Jake was loaded, they spurred the horses out into the yard drawing fire from the house. Now they knew their positions, both men picked their point and shot expertly, quieting the shooters within. Jake counted, three down, two to go and quickly rounded the house to back up his brother. Clint's horse was down and he was defending fire from behind its carcass, he indicated a clump of shrub and a wood pile to the left of the house. Jake jumped from his mount and landed beside him. Cal and Jace Caverson were holding up behind the chopped wood.

"We don't have to finish it this way, Clint!" Cal's tone was still unconvincing. Clint and Jake knew better than to fall prey to banter. Words were useless in their world, cunning and sharp aim was what mattered. Or so Jake thought.

"What do you have in mind?" Clint responded. Jake wondered why his brother was even wasting breath.

"We could work this out financially instead of so...barbarically...." Cal was always using big words, a further waste.

"I won't be bought Cal, this is a matter of rights." Finally Jake saw what was causing Clint's sudden need for conversation, their father moved carefully through the brush behind the woodpile. Clint was trying to distract the Caversons so Lionel Murray could pick them off from behind.

"Oh come on now," Cal mocked, "every man has his price, what would it take to lease water and passage rights from the Murray ranch?"

"A hell of a lot more than you've got, Cal Caverson." The

deep voice answered from behind, Cal spun to meet his would be assailant but before he could shoot, Lionel shot both men dead.

Lionel Murray lowered his weapon, stopping to catch his breath. The ring of gunfire died, the dust and smoke slowly started to clear. Jake and Clint began to pick themselves up, gathering weapons and livery from the downed horse. Another water dispute ended.

An echo from a single rifle shot broke the momentary calm with a clap. The sound stunned all three men, by their count all the Caversons were down, confusion and another rush of adrenaline crossed the brother's faces. They turned to see the shocked look of their father as he fell in slow motion to his knees and then face down on the sandy ground. They scrambled to him, dragging him behind the wood pile.

He groaned as Clint rolled him over, his waistcoat and vest were already soaked a dark sticky red. They both knew he would be dead momentarily. In their haste to reach him neither one had grabbed their weapons, Jake had only his right six-shooter, with only two shots left. They quickly realized that the reason for all the chatter on the Caverson's side of the wood pile, they were out of ammo as well. They sat low with their backs against the split wood and caught their breath.

"Can you see his horse?" Clint referred to Lionel's mount about 50 feet away. Jake nodded.

"I thought we had them, who did we miss?" Both brothers scowled in recollection

"The shot came from the house. I heard a woman, did you kill her?" Jake asked. Clint shook his head 'no'.

"I never saw her. We can get him to his horse, yours

should come by, and we can ride out. If it is a woman she won't come after us. We're finished here."

Clint paused as he stooped over his father's body, out of respect he closed the old man's eyes. There was no time or energy for tears. Jake got under one arm, Clint the other and they fairly flew to their two remaining horses with their father in tow. No more shots came from the house. The Murrays headed back to the barren piece of land they had defended.

Long after the stolen biscuits had been shared and worn off, after hours of riding in the daytime heat, the Murrays passed back through their home ranch gate.

Despite the gnawing in his gut and being caked in dust covered sweat and blood, Jake had spent the day trip deep in thought, making plans. Clint had been silent on the trek back as well, no doubt contemplating his own future. Their father was dead. Lionel Murray was the last of another generation of Murrays that had given their life for this blasted land. Jake didn't know how his brother felt about it all but he would be damned if he would die like the man slung across his saddle.

The ranch was half his. He had made the decision. He would demand his share of its worth in cash and leave this damned place. His brother wouldn't like it, that much he did know, but eventually Clint would be glad to be rid of Jake. Jake would finally be a free man. One more thought had occupied his mind for the better part of the ride. Who was the woman that had fired the single shot from the Caverson's house that had changed his whole life?

5

———

Bev could feel the heat as the patrol car came to a stop with the other official vehicles at the scene. Officer Gant jumped out and disappeared in the distorted light of the fire and emergency strobes. The building was what Bev would describe as engulfed, flames shot out from the second story windows and rolled in waves across the roof. The scene and the heat literally took your breath away. Wood popped, the building groaned, water hissed, the whole image was like a starving beast consuming a stolen meal. Firemen in full garb were spraying in vain at the beast, barely able to direct the force of water to do their bidding. Other firemen aimed at damage control and made sure the beast only devoured what it had in its grasp.

Bev now saw familiar faces, Officer Mac, the Spanish pressman, who Bev knew now as Raul, Elena, her boss Hal Preston, Anne from the library, and basically everyone else in Alpine. Evidently a five-alarm fire was big entertainment.

Her reporting instincts kicked in. She grabbed her digital camera and began taking short video of the fire and interviewing bystanders. Anyone see anything suspicious, who reported the fire, how quickly did the firemen arrive, who owned the building, what was it used for? She would interview the owners and the fire chief when they were less entangled.

The building was one of main street's older structures, had once been an auto repair garage in the 50's and more recently an art studio. It had been vacant for several years. Public opinion was generally "good riddance". It had been an eyesore, a hangout for stray cats and gang members the latter of which, according to some locals, had probably set the fire for fun.

"Kids not the cats," one elderly gentleman joked.

The property owner would be relieved now, he could sell the land. Firemen were certain no one had been in the building, there had been no loss of life, feline or human. All in all, just a hard night's work for the public servants and a bit of excitement for the locals.

The beastly fire fought hard for its life but was rapidly being beat into a heap of black timbers and greasy smoke.

Bev got an official statement from Officer Mac, "Investigation is pending but as of tonight it looks like vagrants or *old* electrical wiring caused the blaze."

Her newest official acquaintance Fire Chief Jesus Martinez, "Thanks to the crew for fast response and containing the blaze to this building. No one was inside, the official cause of the fire will be determined in the investigation to follow."

The owners of the property lived in Austin and could be reached by phone in the morning, or later in the morning. Bev finally looked at her watch when she noticed the moon had set and there was the faint glow of dawn coming over the ridge. It was 3am.

"Wow, I'm going to be tired later," she thought, looking

through the dwindling crowd for her ride. She blinked, not realizing till now how much the smoke had affected her eyes. They were dry and burning. She finally saw him talking to two of the firemen as they loaded supplies back on the truck. They were obviously friends by their easy demeanor with one another. Sam Gant helped them put away equipment, joking with them. He somehow managed to get laughter from his exhausted comrades. The revelry stopped as she walked up. Gant immediately realized that he had shirked his responsibility.

"I'm sorry, Beverly, I completely forgot...." He actually looked flustered. Did she see a chink in the armor? She wasn't sure if she should be proud that she saw a weakness or if she should be offended that she was so easily forgotten. She cut him off.

"No problem, I've been gathering details for my article, I'm just now finishing up myself."

He stared at her for what seemed like an eternity and broke into a silly grin, the fluster was gone.

"Good! Glad to hear you're getting the scoop, by the way this is Marco and Luis, some of Alpines finest. Gentlemen, Mrs. Beverly Connors, Alpine Avalanches newest freelance reporter."

They also grinned silly grins like she had missed the punch line of some off color joke and shook her hand.

"C'mon I'll get you home," Sam Gant turned her with a hand on her shoulder. She had the distinct feeling that the boys in slickers behind her were holding back laughter.

"Men!" She thought and dutifully got back in the police car.

Wow, was she exhausted and hot. She couldn't think of a thing to say on the drive back to Fort Davis and evidently neither could Gant. A simple "Here you are," was all he offered with his boyish grin again as she got out.

"Thanks," she muttered and watched him drive off. She drug herself up the stairs and went straight to the bathroom to find fresh cool water for her face and eyes. It took only a second to figure out what had tickled the cop and the firemen's funny bones. Her face was covered with black soot and her eyes had watered making trickling marks down her cheeks. She looked like a heavy metal band groupie. Had she looked like this the whole time?

"Oh, brother, so much for professional prowess!" She splashed and scrubbed, too tired to care too much. "What infants,' She said with disgust stripping off her clothes and practically falling into bed. As her clean face hit the white fresh pillow she had to chuckle to herself. "A barn burner," she muttered still grinning and fell into a deep dark smoky dream.

6

———

Netty Caverson sat in the sudden silence after the gun fight for what seemed like hours. Her heart slowly stopped pounding in her throat and her breathing slowed. The sting of her wound and the slow realization that no one else stirred brought her out of her shock. She had shot the rifle before at snakes, Mexicans and prairie chickens but she had certainly never killed anyone.

She took a deep breath and pulled herself up with her good arm from under the sink in the kitchen. Her shoulder had been hit but just grazed. The bleeding had stopped, but the sting of gunpowder remained.

The Murrays were long gone, it was mid-day. None of her brothers, her cousin or her father had called out or so much as groaned leaving her to assume they were all long dead and had not suffered. She began to assess the damage, both household and human, caused by the fight.

Several broken dishes in the kitchen, breakfast scattered on the table and floor. Splintered door casings and wall board indicated the front of the house had been well peppered.

Seth and Carson lay at opposite ends of the front room, both shirtless just as they had come to breakfast. Seth still clutched his hand gun, laying face up, half of his head gone, displaced on the walls and floor around him. Carson lay face down, blood pooled around his face and shoulders. She felt a sudden wave of nausea and ran to the front porch to vomit as if she should save the room from mess. Marshall, her cousin lay in the dirt at the bottom of the porch steps and two other laborers lay further out in the yard. The rest of the workers had fled no doubt.

She wiped her face with her apron and walked around the back of the house. Her father and youngest brother would be in the back. She was dreading the sight.

She was middle born in the Caverson brood, Seth and Carson, then her. Jace was her baby brother, more like a son to her. Her mother had died giving birth to him when she was five. She had taken care of him from day one. Her eyes were filled with hot tears by the time she rounded the corner of the house.

Her older brothers and her father had treated her no better, and sometimes worse than the Mexican help, but Jace had loved her and she had loved him as much as any sibling could love another. They had shared childhood secrets, treasures and fun when time afforded. She had taught him to read, he taught her to shoot. He had grown into a fine young man and protected her against the unwanted advances of laborers and even her brothers and cousin as she had blossomed. Jace had promised to take her away to San Francisco, to ride in a carriage, to see the world.

"Oh, Jace," her sobs were wracking her shoulders before she laid eyes on him. "Jace, no!" She ran to him behind the woodpile. Jace lay back as if asleep against the chopped wood, her father lay awkwardly on his side beside him. She brushed her brother's hair away from his young face and lifted his chin. To her, he had always been perfectly beautiful, now dirt and blood splattered his blonde stubble. The wound was to the heart, not much blood. To her amazement he was breathing ever so slightly.

"Oh my God, Jace?" She asked pleadingly. He didn't open his eyes but struggled to move his mouth. "I'm here Jace! I've got you." His mouth curved slightly upward.

"Net?" It was all he could do to whisper half her name.

"Oh Jace," she put her forehead to his. "Please, Jace don't leave me," her tears splashed on his cheeks.

He groaned, and with a final surge of energy, put his hand on her face and said, "Take it and go, Netty." His hand fell solidly to the ground and a shuddering breath left his lips.

"Nooo..." the word was guttural and commanding, "no, please, no!" She took his face in her hands as if to wake him by sheer willpower. It was no use, he was gone.

"Jace," she whispered and kissed his forehead and cheeks as she used to do to sooth him as a child. Sliding beside him, she rested there, her head on his chest, not wanting to go on.

Several hours passed until finally the cold chill of the desert evening forced her up. There would be a lot of work to do in the morning.

NETTY TOOK a deep breath and for the second time in a week took a critical look around the Caverson homestead. This time things were tidy. Dishes packed, floors scrubbed, clothing, bed linens and sundries were all packed in the waiting wagon.

She had spent the past five days burying her family and taking account of all of her father's possessions; land, livestock, guns, tools and equipment. He had been a thrifty man through some intelligence, but mostly theft. There had been deeds for land in north Texas territory that she had never heard of, card game signatures for Mexican workers and the most intriguing, a deed for a hotel in town that he had swindled or killed someone to get. There was some money too, not much, but she would sell the horses and the wagon if she had to.

Jace's last words to her had encouraged and strengthened her as she had worked. She would do just as her brother had told her, take it and go. He had never told her wrong.

She had one thing in particular going for her, not many people knew that Calvin Caverson had a daughter. He hadn't thought it important enough or cared about her enough to share that fact. She had been a burden to him, a liability. She had only been off the ranch as a girl on cattle drives to help cook for the cowboys. It would be easy to erase her father's past and be rid of the Caverson name and its history, no one would be the wiser. She had decided to take her mother's maiden name Bingham from this point forward. No one knew her, no one needed her. Except for the ache in her heart over Jace, she was free.

Netty turned and looked once more. If not for the five new graves that adorned the yard, the homestead would look like it did any other summer day. Hot, desperate, and grey.

"Take it and go, Netty Bingham," she said to herself as she mounted the wagon, tied her bonnet under her chin and set off. Netty never looked back.

7

———

The copy set in a neat pile on Hal Preston's desk by 8:45 Tuesday morning. Bev was in her temporary office working on her version of last night's fire and her historical fire piece, she thought she may be able to tie the two together in a special interest feature if Hal thought it would be newsworthy.

The front door of the paper opened and closed without any ceremony in the reception area other than a muffled good morning. It was Hal. He peeked in the door of her office and grinned.

"Some weekend huh?" He was obviously happy there was some "real" news to report this week.

"Yes, very exciting. I put some copy on your desk for you to look over." He placed a cup of coffee on her desk.

"Thanks! I'll take a look."

As quick as he came he was gone, two strides to his office down the hall.

"I like it here," Bev thought, sipping her coffee.

She hadn't been typing long when the front door opened again. She might have to move offices, this place was like grand central. Elena greeted the visitor casually, she must know him. He rounded the corner without taking note of Bev and went down the hall to Hal's office. It was Officer Mac. She could tell by his step he had some important dealings with her boss. She tried to type but her nosy nature got the best of her and she quit ticking at the keyboard of her computer to listen through the wall.

Being men, their voices were low and hard to understand at first. Something about the investigators findings, the fire. She listened again.

"Just as we suspected," Mac went on. Hal made no audible response. "There is a pattern."

Pattern? Were they still talking about the fire? Bev quietly stood up and went to her door.

"Aha!" Hal's sudden animation made Bev jump back from the door, fearing she had been discovered. But he continued.

"So you're letting me have it?"

Bev was still confused. What were they talking about?

"Yes, all three have the same MO. Acetone with a Molotov cocktail fuse, probably a cotton T-shirt or rag."

Three? Three fires? This was news to Bev. Purposely set fires? Arson? That was news for everyone. She could see why Hal wanted to break the story.

"There doesn't seem to be any connection to the buildings, land or land owners that we can find. The acts seem very random." Mac turned on his cop voice now, "If it's kids I'm going to personally book them, I'm tired of the disrespect from the damn juvenile delinquents."

"Thank God no-one has been hurt," Hal offered. His tone was unconvincingly serious, he sounded like he may even be grinning. The crane snapping at the fish in front of him.

"Mm," Mac stood and Bev jumped back to her desk like a startled cat, bumping her knee on the metal desk.

"Run the story if you want Hal. I'll tell the fire chief to be ready for more. These bastards love the attention of the media. Damn kids."

Mac came down the hall facing her this time. He lifted his hand in a casual greeting, she waved smiling weakly, eyes tearing from her knee injury.

Bev pretended to type, knee throbbing, and listened to Hal. He had begun typing almost as soon as Mac had turned to leave.

"Guess he's taking the scoop for himself," Bev was disappointed, "he is the boss after all."

She resigned herself to the page she was working on in front of her but her mind wandered. She recalled the first time she had seen Hal and Mac at the police station. That was what they were "putting a lid on", that the fires were intentional, possibly arson? Bev didn't remember having to get permission from the police to run stories in Denver, maybe occasionally from the DA on highly sensitive cases. Maybe this was how it was done in small towns for the "protection" of the people.

She tried to brush off the irritation she felt about the paper being subject to the governing law enforcement and the fact that Hal hadn't shared the arson story with her all day, but it wouldn't go away.

Hal stayed in his office typing until early afternoon. She broke for lunch and when she came back he was out and her copy was on her desk with a sticky note attached. It read "great".

What did that mean? Was he running it? And more importantly, where was the check?

Almost as if on eerie mind-reading queue, Elena

stepped in and handed her a business envelope. A check for $250 was inside. Well, now she knew where the bar was for "barn burner."

"Must have to be more than one barn," she said to Elena, who smiled mysteriously and went back to her desk.

"More than one barn," she thought to herself. The rabbit on the trails in her mind ran wild. She wondered where the other two fires were, no one mentioned them the other night as she was inquiring about the current fire. Had no-one connected the dots and thought of arson?

If they had been discussing this the first day she met them then the invaluable Gant knew about the other fires too. Didn't he suspect? Why didn't he mention it to her? I guess he didn't have to tell her anything. After all in the very short time they actually had spent together they had been occupied with other official business, tickets, car break-downs, fires.

Her rabbit trails were leading to one place and she didn't like the idea of following them. She had thus far avoided actually having to ask Gant anything but all arrows were pointing to him and what he already knew. She made a quick call to the police station to find out where to pay her speeding ticket, closed her files on her computer, and headed out the door two blocks to the right to pay her fine and find Gant. Both bitter pills to take.

8

Jacob Murray sat at the well-worn bar at the Longhorn Saloon. He felt like a new man. He closed his eyes and drank his third shot slowly letting it burn the back of his throat. The music from the tinny piano filtered between the sounds of men's voices engaging in loud, laughing conversations. He opened his eyes noticing his reflection in the mirror behind the bar. Hell, he looked like a new man. He was a new man.

After he and Clint had buried their father, Jake hit Clint up for his half of the estate. He wanted cash. Clint had been angrier than Jake had ever seen him. Had called him every name in the book. Jake didn't care, he wanted out. Clint finally agreed to 1/2 on the dollar for Jake's share, keeping Clint from having to liquidate all of this year's cattle crop. That suited Jake fine, he wouldn't have to wait.

The promissory note was written, Jake was packed and moved to town within a week of his father's death. He didn't expect to hear from Clint again. Just as well, there was no love lost there.

Jake had wasted no time getting cleaned up and finding

new lodgings at the local hotel. Now he only needed one more thing to complete his transformation, a new opportunity. He had all the trappings of the man he wanted to be. He had money to invest, and he was certain he could make his fortune with the right opportunity.

He surveyed the crowd. He was making it a habit to know everyone who was anyone in the small western cow town. The more people you knew, and the more you knew about, them the greater your chances of success.

He was also making it a habit to know the lovely ladies of this town. He had always loved to visit the whores when he had time, but now he could afford to be more selective, decide on his favorites and lavish them accordingly.

They had just begun their evening parade down the stairs and his heart fluttered when Janine's ruffled skirt touched the landing. He would inspire her tonight with the gold chain and locket that he had in his pocket and she would purr like a kitten and treat him like a king in one of the feathered beds upstairs. A fire lit in his heart and parts lower at the thought of it.

He bought another round and waited at the bar, she would be by in time. He had bought her services three nights in a row, and she wouldn't pass up a regular paying customer, especially Jake.

The men hooted and threw suggestive remarks around the room as the ladies made their entrance. They patted and played back, advertising their wares expertly. Drinks were poured, cards were dealt, and the evening's festivities began.

Jake watched Janine make her way around the room. She leaned over to look at a card player's hand revealing her beautiful creamy white bosom. His heart pounded at the sight. Someone slapped her rear and she slapped him playfully with her fan. All the while she kept her gaze on Jake in the mirror, slowly teasing him with her banter.

Finally she was behind him, whispering in his ear, nuzzling his neck, pleading with her eyes. It was almost more than Jake could stand. She was so beautiful, not more than twenty, still unlined and firm everywhere. She was perfect. He bought her a drink and lavished in her advances and the anticipation that they brought. Eventually she persuaded him up the stairs to her dark seductive room.

"Oh, Jake, it's beautiful. Put it on me."

She sat up in bed, lifting her brunette hair off her naked back. He slipped it around her neck, kissing her where he fitted the clasp.

She turned over, playfully pulling him to her, the necklace fell perfectly between her breasts. He kissed them too.

"If I didn't know better, I'd say you're smitten with me Jacob Murray," she smiled wryly at him.

"Smitten indeed," he growled pulling her further under him. She laughed and kissed him open mouth and hungry. They both got lost in the touch of bare skin and the big feather mattress.

Later he watched her sleep almost childlike at his side. Her even breathing calmed him and motivated him. Just like Janine, if he was going to get what he wanted he was going to have to go get it. He dressed and made his way downstairs.

Poker games were still being played on two tables, Jake noticed a table with three well-dressed men and an older cowboy. They were just finishing a hand and the cowboy was bowing out.

"Mind if I join you?" Jake asked no one in particular.

"Sure, pull up a chair," the man to his right offered through his clinched teeth where he held a cigar.

Jake extended his hand, "Jacob Murray."

"Dub Masterson," the cigar smoker replied shaking Jake's hand curtly.

He nodded his head to the other players, "Cliff Davis, and Matt Hansen."

"Glad to know you," Jake sat down and loosened his purse strings, settling into the game. By the end of the evening, Jake would have his opportunity.

It took two grueling days for Netty to get to town.

One of the back wheels had come loose from the axle, causing the wagon box to shift, nearly pitching its driver and contents. She had tried to replace the wheel pin herself, which required emptying her belongings and designing a makeshift lever.

After four hours of determined labor, Netty found the wheel too heavy to lift back into place. She sat in the shade of the crippled wagon and considered her options. She could pack everything she absolutely needed on the horses but there were things that had been her mother's, dishes, linens and other household items that she didn't want to give up just yet. She decided to sleep on it. Perhaps she would have the strength in the morning to manhandle the wheel or think of another solution.

She made camp using the side of the wagon to tie a lean to. She cooked cornmeal fritters in a bit of salt pork rendering and rationed her water. All of the excitement and exertion from her first days travel had exhausted her. It took only moments for her to fall asleep as dusk settled over the western horizon.

NETTY'S EYES flew open to the black of the desert night. She wasn't sure if it was the cold of midnight or a sound that awakened her. Her senses told her she wasn't alone. She had no fear of the animals that roamed the southwest, she knew the sounds of the night, but this was someone else moving in the dark, definitely a man. She stayed perfectly still, tightening her grip around her six-shooter that she had tucked beside her bedroll.

The intruder was coming from the other side of the wagon, her horses were tied a few feet away. The sound of his movements were amplified in the thin night air. More than likely he wanted to steal the ponies and would not yet know where she was. He was probably Desert Indian or Mexican. She carefully rolled under the jacked wagon, praying that nothing would shift, collapsing it on her.

Her horses began to prance uneasily at the scent of a stranger. He clucked in hushed whispers to them as he approached. She could barely make out the outline of his lower half moving silently through the brush. He was sandal or bare foot and wore loose ill-fitted clothing. From this angle he didn't look much taller than herself. Surprisingly the horses quieted at his advances. He moved between them and began unhitching them from the shrub where they were tied.

"Ah, Ah, Hombre," her voice seemed to boom in the night air. The thief stopped. She cocked the gun.

"Los manos alto, por favor," he raised his hands as she slid out from under the wagon.

"Estos son mis caballos, Señor. Que pasa?" Her Spanish was passable, not perfect, he would know she was a gringo without seeing her.

"No problema, Señorita, I meant you no harm," his English was thick but also passable.

Hand steady, she continued to aim the gun at his shadowed head. She would shoot him with no regrets.

"Step away from the horses," her tone was direct. Hands still in the air, he moved backwards from between them. "Turn around." Once again he complied but as he turned he smacked one of the horses hindquarters, hollering and waving. Dirt kicked up from the fray sending a cloud around the thief. She shot once, too high though, she didn't want to hit the horses. Suddenly out of the dark, he was in front of her. He was small but had momentum and she was on the ground in an instant, her gun and her horses skittered off into the dark.

Skirts and fists flashed in the thin moonlight. He struck her across the jaw taking the wind out of her, stars danced inside her eyelids for a moment. He was all over her, hot, dusty hands groping. She bit and growled like a wildcat, this would not happen without a fight.

"Now the horses and you are mine, puta," his greasy face was pressed against her ear, he had both of her hands pinned behind her with one of his. She stopped thrashing and saved her energy. He only had two hands and he would have to use at least one to finish what he had started.

He chuckled as she suddenly lay still, misinterpreting her compliance for resignation. As predicted he raised up, attempting one handed to undress them both from the waist down.

She waited giving him time to expose himself. Suddenly, she brought her knee up from behind and between his legs, as fast and as hard as she could, hitting him squarely. He howled, letting her hands loose, grabbing for his groin.

She moved as fast as she could out from under him, her skirts were tangled and it wasn't easy getting upright. She was out of breath crawling across uneven rock and cactus covered ground. He was hurt, but not for long. On his knees he cursed in Spanish, still holding his crotch, he struggled to get up, his clothing also hindering him. Before he could reach down to pull his pants from around his knees, the shot rang out.

There was a shocked cry from the Mexican and he fell face first onto the unforgiving ground. Silence fell, only dust was stirring. Netty could hear her heart pounding and she let out the breath she had been holding. Who? She looked around in vain, there was no light in the brush.

Hot adrenaline driven tears streamed down her face, she had not fired her gun, and she did not know where her gun had gone in the struggle. She moved back to the wagon, backing away from where the shot had come from.

"Hallo!!" A man called from the brush line, not more than 25 feet away, "Is everyone all right?" Netty's senses were acute, she could hear his horse under him, and hers down the hill. She took a chance.

"I'm all right, you shot my attacker, and I believe he's dead." She noticed her mouth was bleeding for the first time. She spat and wiped her face off with her sleeve.

"I'd like to see for myself, may I come into camp?" His voice was surprisingly calm and polite for all that had just transpired. It was deep and assuring, but she was wary. He could be an accomplice. She paused.

"Do you have a lantern?" She had one herself but she wanted the advantage of seeing him without him seeing her.

"Certainly."

A red flash of a flint or a match broke the darkness and in a moment the whole night was lit with a dome of yellow light. He held the lantern above his head, obviously guessing her tactic, showing himself and his mount. He was a broad shouldered man, his mount was saddled in good tack, and he did not look sinister, but in fact comfortable in the dark dessert around him.

"Do I pass?" He looked humbly into the dark in front of his lamp light. She waited, letting her heart slow down, he lifted the lamp higher.

"Yes. Thank you."

He stopped a few feet on the other side of the dead man, dismounted and picked up her gun. He crossed the remaining distance on foot, lantern and reins in one hand. He handed her the gun like a peace offering, gun butt first.

"You put up quite a fight, Ma'am. Are you sure you're all right?" He looked at her in the eyes, past the dirt and blood, looking for the real answer.

"I think so..." she replayed the scene, suddenly the side of her face began to throb, "just some bruises, mostly wounded pride."

"I'm glad I came. I heard a gunshot, got curious. I'm glad I got here in time." He glanced at the corpse. "Why don't you sit down while I get rid of him?"

She gladly let him take her elbow and help her lower to the ground. She felt suddenly shaky and sick to her stomach. He drug the thief into the bushes, his pants still around his knees.

"Fitting," she thought in disgust.

She closed her eyes and took a deep breath. Her horses had made their way back to camp curious to meet the visitor. He tied them up with his.

"Do you have any water?"

"Yes," she began to get up.

"Not for me, for yourself. Don't get up. Is it in the wagon?"

She nodded. He brought a drink from the barrel beside the wagon and offered it to her. She drank, still tasting blood.

"Maybe you should rest, I'll keep an eye on things until morning." He looked genuinely concerned. She decided to trust him, really what else could she do.

"Thank you mister...."

"Murray, Clint Murray, Ma'am" He tipped his hat and if he noticed the shock on her face he didn't let it show. It was a moment before she could return the introduction.

"Netty Bingham."

9

———

"What? 175?! That is literally highway robbery! Can't I take a class or something?" Bev, much to her annoyance, was trying to do her civic duty and pay her speeding fine. Somehow the same stoic Goth young woman from the reception desk at the police station in Alpine had made her way to the courthouse in Fort Davis. Some kind of job rotation no doubt. She stared at Bev blankly.

"No class?! What happens if I want to protest the ticket?"

Goth girl handed her a form. "Still costs $50," she managed to explain.

"Good God!" Bev began filling out the form, "You do take credit cards, don't you?"

Bev's new best friend pointed to a sign taped to a pillar behind the desk "CASH ONLY".

"Crap."

"Is there a problem miss?" Goth girl smiled over Bev's shoulder. Bev recognized the voice immediately. Officer Gant towered behind her.

"Yes, there's a problem! This ticket is the problem! $175!

It's outrageous! And no class and no credit cards! Where am I, the moon?" Officer Gant was grinning as usual. Between Goth girl and Supercop it was like a Cheshire cat convention.

"Well not exactly the moon," he winked at Goth girl. Bev slapped her money and her form on the counter she felt like slapping the grins off of both of their faces.

"Come back in two weeks," mumbled the dumb-struck clerk. Bev stormed out with Gant close behind.

"Really, this is all your fault!" She turned on him at his car.

"My fault? I believe you were speeding!"

"You could have given me a break, a pass. I'm a tourist for God's sake!"

His face changed, "Well, I do feel bad about it when you put it like that." He paused, thinking, "Tell you what, let me make it up to you."

Finally! She was getting through. Thank goodness he was going to expunge the ticket. The sudden act of kindness threw her off her rant.

"Well, Ok then! That's more like it! Do I need to sign something else or something? Let's do it now while we're here," she started to turn back to the courthouse. He caught her arm.

"No, I didn't mean that. I meant, let me make it up to you by taking you to dinner." He grinned questioningly.

"Oh, no way!" She shook her arm loose, "you're asking me out? Now I have to sleep with you to get the ticket erased!" An older woman passing by turned at the comment, Gant waved.

"Man, you're a hot head. Cute, but a hot head! Did I say anything about sleeping with me?" He was trying to diffuse the situation by talking in hushed tones. "I just wanted to go to dinner. I've got to eat, and I assume you've got to eat. I'll even pay, since I know you're a little low on cash at the moment." She glared. "Plus, there is something I wanted to talk to you about." He stood to full height, his grey eyes serious. "These fires." He adjusted his superhero belt at his waist.

Her whole thought process came screeching to a halt. It was exactly what she had intended on talking to him about. She decided not to act too eager.

"The fires?" She played dumb.

"Yes, I need a fresh perspective. Let me tell you all about it over dinner," he glanced around as if there might be someone listening.

"Dinner." She was skeptical, but insanely curious.

"Dinner!" He was wearing his sunglasses low on his nose and wiggled his eyebrows suggestively.

"All right, dinner, to talk fires." She was not amused.

"Great, I'll pick you up at seven, dress casual"

"Like there was any other way here," Bev thought.

He jumped in his car and was pulling away before she could respond again.

SHE FINALLY DECIDED on a black turtleneck, jeans and black "casual" boots. She mindlessly picked up the silver hoop earrings and began putting them on. Her stomach flip-flopped and a flood of emotion came over her.

Ethan had bought her these earrings. They were in Steamboat spending the weekend, one of their first getaways together as a couple, before they were married, before all the problems. She had seen them in the store window as they strolled the streets that evening, he had bounded out of the store with them so proud of himself. She took a deep breath. This would be the first evening out with an eligible man since her divorce. It obviously wasn't a date, but still her emotions were running wild.

"Calm down, for God's sake," she thought, "you're going to dinner with Dudley Do Right. You are going to pick his brain, let him pay for your food...and that's it!"

"Plus, as far as he knows, you're still married," she told herself in the mirror.

She gathered her jacket and purse and headed downstairs. He was waiting in the lobby in front of the fireplace. Despite her best ability she couldn't help but notice how he filled the room with certain security and how his eyes twinkled when he grinned.

"You clean up well, Mrs. Connors. Hungry?"

"Yes, thank you, and so do you Officer Gant."

They were both grinning as they walked out into the cool evening air.

10

_____

Fate was on his side. The cards had been dealt in his favor hand after hand. It was Jacob Murray's lucky night. He had plenty of cash to play with and as the night progressed and the whiskey flowed the other players grew reckless, certain their luck would change. Property deeds and dry goods, even pocket watches became legal tender for their failed card play. By the early morning hours Jacob was sitting amidst towers of chips, legal documents, and angry poker players.

You've had quite a run, Murray." Dub Masterson looked tired and deflated. "You owe me a chance to win back my property."

"Certainly!" Jacob shook his hand as he rose to leave the table, he had no intention of doing any such thing. The other players grumbled as they left with their own intentions of never giving Jacob the chance to whip them at cards again.

Funny, Jacob wasn't particularly good at poker, he took it as a sign that this was the turning point. He took the winnings to his room. Janine was gone, probably working down the hall. Just as well, he wasn't sure he trusted his treasure with her yet. After all she was a whore. He laughed to himself.

He had taken $500 to the table. He had $1279 in cash, a $50 voucher for the mercantile store, a silver pocket watch, a mother of pearl tie tack and a deed for a 12 room hotel in town.

"Interesting," he thought, maybe he could set Janine up as the Madame of her own house.

He could be the master of a bevy of beautiful firm young things paid to do his bidding. The thought was pleasing, he let his mind wander through the fantasy, as he undressed on the side of the bed.

He laid back, "no" he wanted respect and power over men, he already had it over women. He would have to run a legitimate business. Make his money honestly, but spend it wickedly. With wealth he could do as he pleased. This was his dream, to do as he pleased. No one telling him what to do or when or how it had to be done.

He closed his eyes and pictured a fine hotel, the best fixtures and finishes, elegant well to do customers an oasis of refinement in this dust bowl. He drifted off to sleep to images of himself dressed like a gentleman behind a marble counter.

CLINT MURRAY WAS bent over the axle of the wagon when Netty opened the one eye that would cooperate. The other was swelled shut, her jaw was tender to the touch and her head pounded. The Mexican thief had packed quite a punch. She groaned inadvertently as she sat up, Clint turned.

"Don't bother getting up Miss Bingham. It will be a bit before this wagon is ready to roll. Can I get you something?"

Netty's emotions picked up where they left off the previous evening. What cruel twist of fate had made her brother's killer her savior? Clint stood there, looking at her questioning, a picture of innocent chivalry.

"No, thank you, Mr. Murray. I feel I should get up to work out the stiffness." He rushed to her side and helped her up. "Thank you again," she barely whispered, "I think I will go down to the creek."

He let her go and returned to his task. Her head was spinning by the time she reached the muddy water's edge, but not from her physical condition.

She didn't believe much in God, her own father had not put much emphasis on the spiritual things in life and had been a poor example of any faith. In her mind there was no reason to leave vengeance to a higher power. She was torn as to how she should react. If she hadn't recently been slammed in the head perhaps it would be clearer. She knew that any other day her anger to avenge her beloved Jace would have driven her to attack Clint Murray with every ounce of her strength in hopes of killing him on the spot, but something in the concern in his voice and the fact that he had probably saved her life was stopping her.

"What does that mean?" She thought out loud. She continued to ponder as she washed her face in the murky water. Her thoughts cleared as the cool water eased her swollen cheek.

"I will wait. He doesn't know who I am. I need his help. There will be another time, a better time." Netty's heart darkened, she stood, smoothed her skirts and hair and strode up the hill with new determination. She smiled at Clint as he explained what he had done to repair the wagon.

"Take it and go…" Jace's voice kept whispering in her head as she made pleasant conversation with Mr. Murray, helping him with repacking the boxes and making a meal.

"I'm certainly thankful you were out last night Mr. Murray. I thought I could defend myself against anything. I was wrong." Netty could tell the flattery was working.

"I'm glad I came in time Ma'am. Would you like me to ride the rest of the way into town with you? I was going that direction myself." She recognized a look on his face, a longing for attachment.

"I would appreciate it." She sighed. "It would certainly be nice to have company along the way." He smiled broadly, tipped his hat and went off to harness and saddle the horses.

Perhaps there was more of Cal Caverson running through her veins than she wanted to admit, but she found a great satisfaction in playing this role for a greater purpose. She justified every action against her brother's dying breath and felt no remorse.

They left the campsite, wagon intact, Netty at the reins. Clint rode along side, already her protector, defender and – unbeknownst to him – target.

THE TITLE and assayers office was in the center of town. Netty strode confidently along the boardwalk. It had been easy to set Clint to the task of selling the horses and wagon, he was already her large faithful dog.

Their conversation on the half day journey had centered on his ranch and its holdings. She had managed to keep him from asking her too many personal questions. As far as he was concerned she was a woman on her own, vulnerable. She smiled to herself, favoring her sore face, she liked the feeling of this power. She knew women had an aura, a mystique that men could not resist, but she hadn't until now put it to any specific use. It was intoxicating to think of the possibilities.

The small man behind the counter started a bit when she pulled off her bonnet. Her face must be a sight.

"Terribly sorry, I must look a fright. I had a bit of trouble with my wagon on the way into town," she spoke softly, smiling shyly. The clerk's face softened.

"How unfortunate, what can I do to make your day better?" He grinned genuinely. Netty pulled the papers out of her bag.

"Hmm, yes, a property deed, I see," the clerk was mostly speaking to himself. He flattened the papers on the counter, smoothing the creases. He read the text through a monocle.

The office was tiny, two walls covered in small boxes, most of which were stuffed with folded or rolled paper. There was a beautiful scale on the wooden counter, detailed in silver and bronze work. Multiple sizes of lead weights sat on the counter nearby to offset what was alternately weighed on the scale. Netty was fascinated. How quickly the scales were balancing in her favor.

"This is a deed for the old hotel?" The clerk seemed surprised.

"Yes, well actually, I have never seen it. I've come into its possession through my father's estate," she hoped she sounded reasonable. "It will be my only means of making a living. I'm the only living relative."

"I see," he paused looking at her with a puzzled face. "There is a slight problem, Miss Caverson."

"Bingham, Cal Caverson was my step-father." She hoped the lie would hold legally.

"Miss Bingham, the deed states that you are only part

owner." His eye piece made his one eye look three times larger, making him appear like an awkward fish.

"Part owner? Who are the other owners?" She felt a sense of confusion and a sinking panic setting in.

"Just one. The other owner, funny thing is he just recorded his ownership this morning. I don't think he was expecting you to show up, today or ever." He shuffled recent documents finding the one he was looking for.

"So, then how do I proceed?" She had no idea how these things worked.

"Nothing to do really, you record your part of the owner-ship. You meet with your new partner and the two of you work out the details. Perhaps he will buy out your portion or you may decide to work together in some fashion."

She could tell what he was thinking and leveled her gaze at his lopsided stare.

"Who is this gentleman?"

He handed her papers to sign and he busily stamped them.

"A Mister Jacob Murray, Ma'am. Looked to be a man of some wealth. I believe he's the son of the late Lionel Murray."

"Murray?" She drew the name in sharply. The poor clerk, alarmed at her reaction, hurried to be finished with this awkward transaction.

"Let me just change the name on the documents," he muttered as he turned to another desk top.

She could feel the blood drain from her face. "Two of them, both of them," she thought. It was almost too much to bear. The anger rose up helping her regain her composure. The scales had teetered for a moment but the weight of her brother's death balanced her thoughts. By the time the clerk turned back, her resolution had returned.

"How fortunate to have a partner of means, I'm sure we will be able to come to an agreement," she smiled pleasantly at the little man. He handed her the necessary papers and Netty Bingham walked out the door, the walleyed clerk blinking after her.

11

———

"You are a mystery to me Mrs. Connors."

Sam Gant sat across from her in an outdoor pizzeria, long neck beer in his hand.

"Why is that Officer Gant?" She would have normally felt stupid addressing him formally but she had had two beers herself and she was beginning not to care. She smiled.

"Well..." he leaned in toward her and picked up her left hand. "You claim you're a Mrs., yet you have very little to say about Mr. Connors and you don't wear his ring." He examined her ring finger.

"Hmm," she drew her hand back. "You got me officer." She paused for a moment, trying to determine the pros and cons of opening one tiny door to this man. She could come up with no reason, good or bad. "I'm impersonating a married woman."

He laughed and sat back, feigning surprise.

"I'm actually in the process of a divorce, all but the final signatures." Why was she telling him this? It was supposed to be her trump card, but again she didn't care and took another drink.

He sat for a moment contemplating her.

"Hmm," was finally all he offered and took another drink. She left it at that but somehow felt guilty.

"How about you? Married? Divorced? Gay?" He almost choked and laughed out loud again.

"Man, you don't pull any punches do you?" She was getting used to the playful twinkle in his eyes.

"Journalist remember?" She pretended to be ready to take notes on his answer.

"Mm, right. No, no and no. Haven't had time. I am a super busy public servant."

"Yes, super busy arresting poor tourists."

"Are you on that again? Remember this," he gestured to the patio and table, "is supposed to make up for all that."

"Oh right, I'll try not to mention it anymore."

The waitress came and went, leaving the pizza. For a few moments they busied themselves with the food and drink. He was easy company, easy to look at, polite. Why was he still single, she wondered? There probably weren't that many eligible bachelors way the hell out here, certainly there were some women in this town that could turn a cop's head. She knew that Goth girl liked him. Maybe there was something horribly wrong with him, he lived with his mother, had inherited his father's extra small private parts or worshiped the devil on moonless nights? None seemed likely. Once again she wondered why she cared. They laughed and ate and shared benign personal information with each other until most of the clientele had left.

It wasn't until after the dishes were cleared and they sat over cups of coffee that he brought up the topic she was waiting for.

"So, Beverly, you seem like an astute person."

"Thank you," she raised her empty beer bottle in agreement. He sounded suddenly serious and uncharacteristically nervous, she quit fooling around.

"I think you may be able to see this problem more objectively than most," he glanced around.

She waited.

"I take it you know the fires have been purposely set?" He leaned in and lowered his voice. She met him half way and nodded.

"Yes, three right?"

"Yes," he played with his coffee cup.

"Started the same way, acetone Molotov cocktail," she stirred her own cup.

"Yes, Mac thinks it's kids."

"But you don't."

He shook his head "no" and took another sip of coffee. He waited until another couple who were getting up to leave had gone through the door.

"I think they were set for another reason other than property destruction."

"Like what?"

Arsonists often set fires just to see the flames, to feel the power they had over inanimate objects, some actually got off on fire sexually. She was curious what his theory was.

"Attention," he said suddenly. His theory sounded flat. She furrowed her brow.

"Well, of course it could be for attention, I think I've heard of arsonists returning to the fire just to see the uproar they cause and to tempt getting caught. That wouldn't be an unreasonable assumption–"

He cut her off, "No, not exactly attention, more like publicity."

"Publicity?"

He'd stumped her.

"I can see for insurance money, or for a grudge in a divorce or for a neighborhood dispute, but I don't see publicity."

She let him explain.

"What if a local, who made his living say in tourism or some such was setting the fires to get attention from media, getting Alpine's name on the map?"

"Hmm, I suppose, but why would that draw a crowd of tourists?" He sat back and thought through his theory again.

"I don't know. I was hoping that you, being a tourist, could tell me," he said it half in jest, smiling.

She tried to process his line of thinking. It wasn't coming together.

"I just have a feeling that there's something more to these fires than rowdy kids. My gut tells me there's more to the story. Someone local is gaining something from all this, I just haven't figured out who or why." He looked frustrated.

"That's where the journalist comes in, at who and why," she offered. "I'll think about it and keep my eyes and ears open." For some reason she felt compelled to assure him, "There is one thing I wanted to ask you." His face prompted her to continue, "When I came into the police station that first day and you and Preston and Mac were having your pow-wow, were you talking about the two previous fires?"

"Yes."

He didn't act as though there was anything to hide.

"Is it customary for the police to squelch the printing press here?" The bite in her voice was unintentional. Old 1st amendment crap surfacing. It took him a moment to process her tone.

"Ohhh, no, no you got it all wrong. Mac didn't want to have copycat fire starters setting the town on fire. He just wanted to keep a lid on it until they were sure it just wasn't a fluke. Preston was pissed, but it all worked out." He didn't seem offended in the least by the interrogation. She believed him and felt better. "I'm sure old journalism habits die hard." He winked, "Shall we?"

BEVERLY'S RUNNING footsteps were silent in the snow, she carried the train of her dress in her arms. How could she be late? She was such a fool. She burst through the back doors of the church. The lights were dimmed, candles burned at the altar and along the isle. Her Father greeted her silently, offering her his arm. Thank God she had made it.

They turned and started down the aisle between the old oak pews. She could see Ethan's silhouette waiting at the altar, it was their wedding day. She was so happy, rushed, but happy. A song played on the organ, they were walking so slowly. As they approached she realized there was someone else at the altar, the preacher? No, a female form, standing where she should be, a wave of panic came over her.

No. She tried to speak but there was no audible sound. No, Ethan, it's not me! She wanted to scream, he was marrying someone else, and she was too late! She tried to pull her Father faster but he wouldn't move. When she turned to beg him to hurry, he was gone. She was all alone. She was running down an aisle that kept getting longer. Ethan turned to kiss his new bride, pulling up the veil.

He drew the woman to him and kissed her. Beverly cried out, "Please!" She fell at the foot of the alter looking up at the happy couple as they turned to face the front. Ethan was smiling from ear to ear, his new bride wore a more frozen expression. She was a doll, a manikin. There was a striking resemblance, in fact she looked just like

Beverly. No, Ethan. Beverly began to cry. It's not me, it's not me.

Beverly jumped with a start, her face was wet, she had been crying in her sleep. She sighed and relaxed back into the pillows.

"Oh my God," she wiped her face. She replayed the dream. Could it be that obvious? Her marriage had been based on what Ethan had thought she was? Not the real her? Had she tried to tell him? To show him? Why was it entirely up to her? Could he not see the real her? Love the real her? What was wrong with the real her? What did people really see when they saw her? Why couldn't her Dad help her? She started crying again. Why did everything have to be so hard?

She continued crying for a while, it felt good. She didn't need any other reason, but she added her divorce and her Father's death to the list just for good measure. She was sniffing curled up in the bed when the phone rang. She wiped her eyes, took a deep breath and answered.

"Hey?" At first the casual tone caught her off guard, it was Sam.

"Sam! Hi!" She tried to brighten her voice and sound pleased, she really felt drained.

"You all right?" It pissed her off that he could hear the falter.

"Of Course! What's up?" How did he get this number?

"Just wanted to tell you that I had a good time last night." He was driving, she could hear the cop radio feedback.

"Thank you, me too." She meant it. She had enjoyed his company.

"I was wondering if you were up for a repeat performance." She could imagine the twinkle in his eyes as he asked. A flood of emotion choked her answer. She didn't have the strength for this right now. She was silent trying to hold back another flood.

"Hello?"

"Sorry, I'm here." How could she say this, "Look Sam, I like you but I think we should keep this professional." Her head started to throb, it was his turn to be quiet. The radio was squawking again in the background.

"Ok," he finally replied. "Maybe we can do lunch or something. You know where to find me if you change your mind." He sounded genuinely disappointed.

"Thanks, Sam, see you."

"Bye"

Beverly flopped down and cried some more.

12

The bruise was fading, the swelling nearly gone. Netty had not seen her reflection in a real mirror until she had taken a room in the hotel. Her mother had used the river, a reflection off a platter, or a shiny bit of brass on a saddle, they had never owned a mirrored piece of glass.

She turned, admiring her naked body. She was thin but soft in the right places it seemed. Despite the harsh environment she had been raised in, her skin was bone china white in most places. She had burned her neck and hands traveling for lack of a proper hat and gloves, but the pink tint was fading. Her hair was golden, unusual in this part of the world, everyone here was dark; skin, eyes and hair all the color of brown paper and oil cloth.

Her bright blue eyes were set off by the red drapes behind her. Her dress should be red, she decided. She had waited the week out, trying to stay out of the public eye as much as possible. She wanted to make an entrance, or in reality a scene, at her first public outing.

She had identified Mr. Jacob Murray and watched his

habits. He was very busy flaunting his good fortune. He wasn't bad looking. Thinner and smaller than his brother, but better dressed and more animated. He had an affinity for whores, one in particular. Netty was sure she had the looks to draw his attention if not the skills.

He was planning a public dinner at the hotel for all interested "ladies and gentlemen" to unveil his new hotel plan. The assayer's clerk had not tipped her hand and she planned on making her partnership known at the meeting with Clint on her arm. What better way to introduce their business deal, with witnesses.

She laid out a deep red dress with a touch of golden lace at the collar. She had bought several necessary items at the dry goods store, things every girl needs. Face powders and creams, toilette water and bath salts, all tricks of the trade. She had come a long way from the ranch and intended to live as such.

Clint had agreed to meet her for dinner. He had no idea of his brother's expose' or her partnership in the hotel. He was a bit player, a necessary place holder. She filled her tub and began to dress for the evening's performance.

HEADS TURNED as the strange young woman glided down the stairs and into the lobby of the dining hall. She was dressed in red which accented her golden hair, blue eyes and ivory skin. A beauty indeed. Men and women both turned to companions and whispered.

"Who is she?"

"Do you know her?"

Netty drank in every scandalous word as if energized by the attention. Clint was in the dining hall, luckily he had picked a table to the back. She did not want Jacob Murray to see her too soon in the evening. She almost regretted wearing the red dress but only until she saw heads turn in the dining hall as well.

Clint stood as she approached, his hat in hand, a dumbstruck look on his face.

"A love struck pup," she thought. Everyone stared as he took her hand in greeting.

"Miss Bingham, I had no idea, I mean, you look lovely. Thank you for joining me for dinner," his brown cheeks blushed.

"My pleasure, Mr. Murray. I have been looking forward to our meeting again." He helped her sit in the chair across from him.

They made polite conversation as soup was served. Other diners gathered, filling the room with pleasant murmurs. The hype of Netty's identity seemed to be calmed by her association with Clint Murray. They had just been served their entrée when she noticed a sharp change in Clint's manner. His eyes narrowed and his back stiffened. She saw hate cross his face. Forgetting her manners she turned to see the source of his changed demeanor. At the other end of the dining room stood Jacob Murray.

She looked at Clint again to be sure she read the emotion correctly. She was not mistaken, the brothers were estranged.

"Do you know that gentleman?" She asked coyly.

"That is no gentleman, Miss Bingham. That is my brother," his tone was flat and harsh, it excited her. For the first time since they had met she had some minor respect for Clint Murray. There was fire there after all.

"Forgive me for asking, but what could cause such feelings between brothers?" If she continued to stir his passion where might it lead?

He was about to answer when Jacob Murray called for attention in the room. All the guests turned their attention.

"Welcome ladies and gentlemen. Thank you for coming out tonight for the unveiling of what will be this town's most elegant hotel, no offense Charles," Jacob slapped Charles Worthers back, the proprietor of the hotel where they were all gathered.

"None taken," said Charles.

"This new hotel will draw the wealthiest travelers headed west to San Francisco or east to New Orleans. It can only benefit our town to have two fine establishments."

The crowd mumbled, uncertain. Jacob read their mood and with a showman's flare pulled the veil off the drawing board at the front of the room. The image was striking. White pillars in front of a two-story hotel, a large portico in front. A cut glass lantern hung from the grand entrance ceiling. Netty thought she had never seen anything so beautiful or elegant. She couldn't have imagined it any better herself. All those dreams of carriage rides and fine living suddenly where sketched out in front of her.

"Wonderful!"

"How Lovely!"

The general consensus in the room was changing. All except Clint Murray who continued to fume at the back table, forced to listen to his fool brother's plan to squander their family money.

"As sole proprietor I intend to begin...."

Netty determined this was her queue. She stood and cleared her throat. Clint stood too, confused.

"Excuse me, Mr. Murray."

When Jacob Murray turned to see who was stealing his

moment it was if he had been physically struck. There was the most blindingly beautiful woman he had ever seen petitioning his attention.

"Yes, Miss?" He began to cross the room to her as if by magnetic pull. The red dress was working.

"Bingham, Netty Bingham."

He reached for her hand and nearly recoiled as he suddenly noticed his brother standing behind her. Jacob paused for just a moment then, ignoring Clint, took her gloved hand and kissed it.

"Miss Bingham, a pleasure to meet you." He looked up at her under his long lashes with eyes of a predator.

A wolf, she thought, a handsome wolf.

"Now what question do you have for me concerning my new hotel?"

He kept his eyes on her continuing to ignore his brother. Netty could feel the heat from Clint's anger radiating from across the table.

"Perhaps we should meet in a less public setting, my business is somewhat personal," she looked around at the attentive room, playing her role perfectly.

"Nonsense, we're all friends here," he glanced up for a split second at his brother.

"Very well," she turned and took the newly altered deed from her bag. "I believe you are not the only one who can lay claim to the hotel."

She paused and handed him the papers. Murmurs filled the room once more. His countenance changed in a split second from confusion to anger and back to congenial host, as he quickly scanned the document. He took the papers back to the front of the room as he studied them.

"Please, Miss Bingham, won't you join me?" The wolf grinned a charming grin.

She started forward but Clint grabbed her arm. Her heart skipped a beat–she had them both. Clint looked at her, imploring her.

"You cannot trust him," he said quietly, "don't go, Netty."

"Take it and go," whispered Jace's voice. She smiled and patted his hand, loosening his grip.

"Thank you, Mr. Murray. But I must." She walked to the front of the room and stood next to Jake.

"It has come my attention that I have a partner in ownership of the new hotel!" Gasps and muffled voices filled the room. "May I introduce Miss Netty Bingham."

The room was still and then several men began to clap followed reluctantly by their wary wives and dinner partners. Jacob leaned into her ear.

"I look forward to our partnership, Miss Bingham," his breath was hot and sweet, his nature demanding. Netty was going to enjoy this play she felt certain.

She never noticed that Clint had walked out the door. Her defender and protector had turned tail and left her to the wolf.

13

Bev's week had been busy. She finished the article on the crooked car dealer and another on the new art instructor at Sul Ross. Hal accepted both and she doubled her income for the week. She decided that she should find more permanent accommodations.

After looking at every available rental in the county she settled on a one bedroom studio that was off main street Fort Davis. It was an addition to an old adobe store front that was currently a used clothing store. Not particularly glamorous but maybe she could get free or cheap clothes as a bonus. Plus the rent was a cheap $300 a month, there was a fridge and a stove and her phone worked.

She hadn't seen or heard from Officer Gant since their last phone call. "Licking his wounds", she thought. She pondered the complications of relationships as she walked back from the grocery store.

Suddenly, Hal Preston pulled up beside her in a faded green VW Van, the image was almost too cliché. His long hair was blowing in the breeze.

"Hey Connors!" His long arm flapped out the window. "Need a ride?" It was nice to be recognized.

"Sure," she walked around the passenger side and hopped in. "Thanks, it's not far, but I bought more than I intended."

He pulled out on the main road and headed into town.

"I found a place behind the second hand store."

He nodded knowing exactly where she meant, "Glad you found something suitable. You shouldn't have any trouble paying bills with the work you're turning in. Loved the piece about Clark Auto." When he turned and grinned she was amazed at how attractive he was. She hadn't noticed before.

"Thanks! This is really retro," she admired the van.

"Ha ha! I don't know, somehow it just suits me."

"I agree." They pulled up in front of her porch. "Want to come in for a beer?" She offered.

He cocked his head characteristically, "Sure!" He grabbed one of her grocery bags and they met at the door. He had to stoop to go in. They took the beers outside in the cool evening air.

They talked easily about the paper, their professional histories, and 1st amendment issues. He told funny stories about local characters. She told stories about "big" city papers and politicians. The evening quickly slipped into night.

"My God it's late," he finally offered.

"Yes, I guess it is." They stood together, looking up at the incredible night sky. Bev was a little tipsy, "This was fun Hal, will you come by again?"

"Sure," he grinned, bent down, and kissed her on the cheek then virtually leaped into his van.

"Be careful driving home, Officer Gant is on patrol." She

felt suddenly guilty for saying his name. Hal waved, backed out onto the road, and headed back to Alpine.

Bev wondered if sleeping with your boss would be offensive in this small town. Then she laughed and snorted at the same time as she picked up the empty beer bottles.

"I have got to stop drinking on these dates, it only leads to loose morals." Then she laughed out loud again and went inside.

SATURDAY DAWNED CLEAR AND BRIGHT. Bev woke to the sound of the courthouse clock chiming 8am. She had left her windows open and the fresh morning air drifted in on a soft breeze. She had slept soundly, finally a reprise from disturbing dreams and flashbacks. What a great day to take a hike, get out in this beautiful rugged countryside.

She dressed in her running suit and her best tennis shoes, packed a back-pack, dawned a Rockies baseball cap and headed to the nearby state park. There were plenty of trails to choose from. She headed out on a ten mile loop that would take her to the top of Sleeping Lion Mountain. The ranger had told her that it was the best view of Davis Valley to the south, a great day hike. Perfect!

She traversed up the side of the rocky mountain, keeping a fair pace. There were a few campers in the park but she met no one on the trail. She did startle a horny toad and she noticed three deer making their way down the hill to the river below.

Temperatures were rising fast in the valley she could see the heat waves shimmering, but the air was still cool and there was a breeze as she reached the top. The thick perfume of juniper, cedar and sage filled the air. She paused to take in the view.

It did not disappoint. She must be able to see for a hundred miles or more. The scenery looked like a magnificent backdrop on a huge outdoor stage.

She took a drink and a deep breath. This was a great work out, she would remember it for future outings. It appeared that this was the highest point on the loop, the rest of the trail meandered back down the valley beside the creek and back around to the park.

To commemorate reaching this soaring vista, she decided to get out her camera and take a few pictures. It would be nice if someone was on their way up to snap one of her with the valley in the background. She glanced down the deserted trail and decided she could do it herself.

She moved out onto a protruding boulder to position herself with the valley behind her. She extended her arm and took the shot. Crap, the first shot missed her entirely. She lowered her aim, took another. She took several more, not realizing that each time she was moving step by step closer to the edge. The last shot she took she turned a bit too suddenly and nearly lost her balance.

"Oh my God," she chided herself, "That's all you need, to fall off a cliff!" She slowly eased away from the edge. Just as she thought she had solid footing, her shoe slipped on the loose sandstone and she began to fall.

"No!" She said out loud as if the mere command could keep this tragedy from happening. But it didn't. There was nothing to regain her footing on and she fell hard on her shoulder, sliding down the side of the boulder that she had just been standing on. She struggled to get a foothold or to grab something to stop the fall, she was gaining momentum and would be hurled over the edge if she didn't stop.

Her knee slammed into another large rock, she could feel the smaller gravel and thorny plants scrape her hands and forearms. Dust was flying and then as suddenly as she had tripped she came to a thudding stop.

"Ohhhww!" She yelled, waiting for her head to stop reeling.

She lay very still for a moment, letting her heart slow, assessing her body. Head and neck were fine, her hands and arms and shoulder were scraped, but nothing broken. She could breathe without pain, no broken ribs. When she finally reached her legs she knew in a second that she had either broken or dislocated her knee on the right leg. The pain was searing. Lastly she had lost her left shoe and although the ankle didn't seem broken it throbbed angrily.

How far had she fallen? Fifteen, twenty feet? My God she was lucky to be alive.

Her knee really hurt, tears welled up from pain and anger. How could she have let this happen? She looked around. She had indeed fallen about twenty feet. She was on a ledge under the large boulder that she had been taking pictures on. If she could stand she could climb back up but both her knee and her foot were telling her otherwise. Had she fallen on the other side of the boulder she would have missed the ledge and would now be buzzard food.

She took a deep breath and tried to think rationally about survival skills her dad had taught her. She knew her injuries and her surroundings. It wasn't quite noon, the ranger wouldn't be missing her for another few hours. Her backpack was up on the trails edge, she thought. She had her camera, which she must have had a death grip on during the slide and a half bottle of water that was in her jacket pocket. Her phone was in the backpack, not that it would do her any good. There would be shade soon, cast from the boulder, she sat up and drug herself closer to its protection.

God her knee hurt.

"Shit, I was having such a great day," she told herself.

She laid her head back on the boulder and rested trying not to move except for her even breathing, Being calm and still could increase survival chances, using minimal energy and losing minimal moisture was the best bet.

She recalled another weekend that she and her dad were forced to use survival skills. They had back-packed up to one of the cirque lakes on the western slope in Colorado. She was ten and angry that her dad had made her wear hiking boots. She had trudged behind him. How he loved the outdoors.

They had made camp that night, gone to bed with no real incident, only to wake to three feet of new snow. The trail was gone, everything looked completely different. Large spring flakes continued to fall, making the sky disorienting. He had decided that she would have to stay in the tent while he made ever widening circles around the camp until he came across the trail.

He seemed to be gone forever and at one point Bev had feared he was lost in the blizzard. She was terrified. She had melted snow for the canteens and packed her back-pack in anticipation of having to go find him. Suddenly his silver head dripping wet thrust through the tent door.

"I found it!" He beamed. They had bundled the camp and themselves and headed back down the mountain. How thankful she had been to have the warm hiking boots then. She had gladly put her every foot-step in his.

"My hero," she thought to herself.

The thought of that morning made her shiver. She was

probably going into shock. At least she wasn't bleeding and she did have a jacket on. She tried to concentrate on the heat of the rock at her back to keep her warm. Her adrenaline waned and at one point she dozed off.

When she woke up the shade of the boulder covered all but her feet. She reached down and took off her left sock. The ankle was black and blue and swelled to twice its normal size. She was desperately thirsty and drank all but a couple of swallows of her water. It had to be past 2pm just a couple more hours and someone would miss her...surely. She listened for any sound from above, calling out several times and listening intermittently.

Nothing.

She shifted trying to get more comfortable. Her knee shouted in disagreement. To take her mind off the pain she looked through the pictures on her camera. The self-portraits of her and the vista were poor, all this and not even a good picture. She quickly went back. There were a couple of shots of the rentals she had been contemplating, then the fire shots of the last arson fire.

The arson fire. Her mind desperate to escape the moment began to contemplate. Who was setting the fires? It had to be kids. But something in her gut made her question that theory like Sam. A local? Sam Gant, she saw his concerned face, he was worried about the town, about its people, about her, about a villain on the loose. She saw another face of his, laughing easily, eyes twinkling. She would get back to her historical piece when she got to work tomorrow. Work. Hal. She saw his face. The long chiseled features, long hair flowing in the wind.

"I'm delusional," she said out loud. Where the hell was everyone? The breeze came up the canyon, hot. She should rest some more. She laid her head back on the rock. She didn't think she had been asleep long when a scattering of gravel fell off the boulder above.

She heard voices.

"Beverly!"

"Beverly Connors!"

There were several voices from above. Her throat was dry but she managed to yell back, "Down here!! I'm down here!!"

There was more gravel and sliding stones coming down from the direction she had fallen. Thank God, she thought, her knee and her ankle throbbed and her head hurt.

"My God, Bev!" Sam Gant rushed to her from amidst the dust cloud. "Where are you hurt?" The fear and concern was easily read in his eyes.

"It's my right knee and left ankle."

"Going to need a basket down here," he hollered over his shoulder. She was so glad to see him she almost started crying.

"It was so stupid," she started.

"Don't worry about it now, let's get you out of here, then you can tell me all about it." He gave her water and two mountain rescue workers also appeared at her side as a basket was lowered over the edge of the boulder. She lay back and let them work.

She didn't realize until she was in the basket and being taken up the rock face, when she had to let go of Sam's hand, that she had held onto him the whole time.

"Meet ya at the top," he said as he let go, smiling.

There were more rescue workers at the top as well as the park ranger and Hal Preston. She felt a wave of emotions, embarrassment, relief, exhaustion. Hal walked beside her on the way down, Sam followed at her feet. Both men looked hot, tired, worry worn and serious.

There was an ambulance waiting at the bottom of the trail. Hal jumped in the back with her. She raised up to say thank you to Sam, but he had already turned to his patrol car and the ambulance door shut.

14

"Well, who the hell is she?" Janine had hopped out of bed and was sitting naked at the vanity, angrily combing out her long hair.

Jake sat up against the headboard and lit a cigar smiling. Janine had noticed him spending time with Netty Bingham these past weeks.

"Ahh, jealous." It was a statement.

He couldn't blame her, Miss Bingham was a delicate spring flower compared to the dusty withered cactus blooms here in this town. Janine glared at him in the mirror. He admired her rump on the brown velvet seat and enjoyed the cigar.

"I just don't see why you have to spend so much time with her," Janine pouted professionally.

It would have worked on most men she attended, but not on Jacob.

"I told you. She's my business partner, nothing more."

He closed his eyes letting the fragrant smoke fill his nose and throat. "God, women are predictable," he thought.

"What about our 'business'?" She threw the double meaning at him through perfect rose petal lips.

"What about it?" He puffed casually.

"I thought you and I were partners." She turned and he could see one side of her beautiful breast, she noticed where his eye lingered and put on her satin robe.

"We are partners! Bed mates! That's our business!" He was slightly annoyed at her covering up.

"You told me you would take care of me, that I would have a place in your new hotel!"

How he hated when women remembered pillow talk promises.

"Well, that's changed." He closed his eyes again avoiding her stare.

She was silent for a moment. He waited, maybe she was finished.

"Are you telling me that she will be running the hotel with you?" She said the words slowly, her next actions depending on the answer.

"Yes! Shit, Janine! Did you think I could have a whore at the front desk?"

When he finally had the nerve to open his eyes and meet her gaze, there were tears in them. Angry tears, hate filled tears, wounded tears pooling under her dark brown eyes.

"Get out," she threw his suit at him. "Get out!" She screamed throwing his boots at him.

He dodged as they hit the head board.

"Wait..." He clamored out of bed trying not to set the mattress on fire, "Janine..."

"Jacob Murray, our business is finished, get out!"

There were no tears in her eyes now, her tone was icy.

"Janine! You can't be serious." He gathered his clothes on

the bed, he turned to her nude and in need, excited by the fray.

His grin and bravado quickly fell as he was met with the barrel of her hand gun pointed at his forehead. He raised his hands, mocking her, she lowered the gun to his groin and cocked it.

"Shit, Janine! Fine!" He jumped into his trousers and hurried out the door.

He turned to implore her once more and the oak door slammed in his face.

"Whore," he muttered taking his things back to his own room, cigar still in his mouth and tipping his hat to another man in the hall who noticed his situation.

Netty opened the letter carefully. It had been delivered to the hotel front desk that afternoon. It was from Clint Murray. He had strong, even handwriting and although book learning wasn't her strong suit, she managed to read the inked words on the page.

Dear Miss Bingham,

Please forgive my poor manners in writing to you without asking your permission first, but I feel very strongly about you and am concerned for your safety.

I wish to warn you once more about my brother, Mr. Jacob Murray. He has proven time and time again to be self-serving and without any compassion. He has taken his inheritance from our family ranch to spend on women and gambling. I fear he will use your partnership to his own advantage and may hurt you in the process. I cannot bear the thought of that happening.

I hope you will agree to see me again when I am in town next, however, I do not know when that will be. The ranch is experiencing a drought and my hands and I will be bringing the cattle in earlier than expected this year.

I will eagerly wait for your response. Please be careful.

Your Servant,
  Mr. Clint Murray

"My servant, indeed," thought Netty.

She felt pity for Clint Murray. She wasn't sure about his part in this performance but she thought it best to keep him in the play.

Thus far Jacob Murray had been nothing but cordial, encouraging and professional. They had worked out several details of the hotels design, its financing and its future management in their few first meetings. She saw nothing of the callous, selfishness that Clint spoke of in his brother. He was clever, funny, driven and alluring. Her purpose was still clear, but what was the harm of enjoying the journey? She found her writing paper and pen and returned Clint's letter.

Dear Mr. Murray,

There was certainly no offense taken from your letter. I appreciate your caring for me enough to inform me of Mr. Murray's nature. I will certainly take your advice and guard myself. As of late, he and I have been able to agree on all of our business and foresee a promising future for the hotel.

I would enjoy seeing you again as well. Please contact me when you are in town next. I also feel a very strong bond between us. After all, I owe you my very life and I will never forget that.

Affectionately,

Netty Bingham

"So the play continues," she thought to herself. She gathered her things and carefully folded and sealed the letter. She would post it on the way to meet Clint's brother.

15

The headline read *Local Journalist Rescued from Fall*, pretty standard.

"Oh brother," she said out loud. She was reading the copy when Hal stepped in the room.

"Good you got a copy! Front page!" He grinned and handed her a coffee.

"Great. I feel like an idiot." A dislocated knee, twisted ankle and multiple cuts and abrasions would be a reminder of her idiocy for a while.

"Oh, don't worry about it, you know what they say...'today's news is tomorrows fish paper, or bird cage liner or mulch' or something like that." He sat on the edge of the hospital bed, "How long till you get out?" He watched her carefully, to the point of almost making her uneasy.

"Tomorrow. But the cast and crutches are mine for a glorious six weeks! Don't worry, I can be back at work–"

"Oh no, no, don't worry about that. I was wondering for another reason. You can e-mail me any copy for this week. No biggy," he smiled

"Good thing I did two articles last week and have

provided you with a headline story for this one. What other reason?" She thought she already knew, but she wanted him to say it.

"Well, I've grown accustomed to your face and I miss you and I want to continue what we started last week," he grinned foolishly this time and she grinned back.

"I want that too."

"I'm so glad you're all right," he held her gaze and leaned in and kissed her. She was surprised, but pleasantly.

"Hmhm", Officer Gant cleared his throat in the doorway. Hal and Bev turned to him. He was holding a bouquet of wild flowers that he let fall to his side at the sight of them together.

"Hi Sam!" Hal said a little too assuredly.

"Hal, Beverly."

He handed her the flowers awkwardly.

"Thanks," she gestured for him to sit. "Please stay a minute, I haven't gotten to thank you for finding me." He sat on the edge of the too small hospital chair and took his cowboy hat off.

"How are you feeling?" He played with the brim of his hat nervously. He seemed out of sorts.

"I'm good. Only one dislocated knee and one twisted ankle! Thanks to you."

He relaxed a bit.

"Hey, I've got to get back to the office," Hal suddenly stood. So did Sam.

"Don't leave on my account," Sam stated. There was something smoldering in the comment, but Bev couldn't tell what it was. Hal didn't notice.

"No, no," he said to Gant, "you stay here and visit." To Bev he offered, "I'll see you later," bent way over and kissed her on the forehead, then went lunging out of the room. Bev still wasn't used to the way that man covered distances.

Sam remained standing.

"Please, sit for a while, the walls are so white here I'm about to go nuts. You're a pleasant distraction!" He smiled, but only politely.

"I'll be forever grateful," she started. He began to say something about it being his job. "No, I mean it. Thank you Sam," her sincerity broke through the shell and a spark shone in his grey eyes.

"You're welcome," his sincerity moved her as well. They both paused a moment, unsure where to go next.

"So, I owe you one!" She chimed, interrupting any serious thought they may have had. "What will it be Officer Gant?" She playfully prompted him.

"Hmm," his humor seemed to return and he pretended to rub his chin and think deeply about his choices. Finally he leaned in towards her bed and raising his eyebrows said, "Take me to dinner." His eyes twinkled happily like a cat with an injured mouse.

She leaned back, she hadn't really expected him to take the offer.

"What the hell," she thought, "he did rescue me."

"Ok. Dinner. When I get back on my feet."

He stood, patting her hand on the bed. His grey eyes had a different look in them than she had seen before. She couldn't quite read them, relief maybe?

"I'm glad I found you," he paused long enough for her to hear a deeper meaning in the comment, then he was out the door.

～

NEGOTIATING crutches was harder than she remembered. Bev decided to stay at home for the better part of two weeks, giving her weak ankle longer to heal to support her even weaker knee.

"What a mess you've made for yourself, Connors." She had started talking to herself just to hear a human voice in the house, which was beginning to concern her.

She had been able to work from home. Hal would bring her leads on stories, coffee and Ben and Jerry's Ice cream and she would email him her story copy. Their relationship was growing steadily. He was funny, intelligent and thoughtful, if not a little assuming and slightly pushy. Nothing that really bothered Beverly, yet.

They had been forced to take their physical relationship a little slow due to her cast, which surprisingly didn't bother Beverly either. She was attracted to him but somehow not overly anxious to jump in the sack with him, when she was sober at least. She got the definite opposite feeling from him. He was chomping at the bit!

"Just going to have to slow that pony down," she thought aloud again. Maybe she needed a pet.

She returned her focus to her historical piece. Being forced to sit still had allowed her to do a lot more reading about the fires of 1881 and the histories of the families involved.

A regional drought had caused several ranchers in the outlying areas to bring their cattle into town to stock watering tanks. The city, staying true to any governing body, had taken "the opportunity" to propose a per head watering fee. Of course the cattlemen were not happy about this and began first legally, then not so legally, disputing the cities ordinances.

One family name kept coming off the pages. Murray.

There was a Murray on the city's side and a Murray on the rancher's side. Brothers.

"That must have made for some fun filled holidays," the talking to herself was so common place now, she was ignoring it.

There was a tin-type photograph of the two men and a blonde attractive woman at the opening of the Belle Hotel. By their faces there was no love lost between the men. Why would they be in the picture together? Was the woman their sister? Certainly not their mother! What would cause two grown men who hated one another to pose for a photo together?

"Only a woman," she looked closer at the photo. The smaller man held the woman at the waist, pretty intimate for back then. The larger man stood at her side, stern, like a sentry. The woman was stern too, but beautiful. There was a steely look of satisfaction in her eyes.

Bev's imagination ran wild. What if both the Murray's were in love with this woman? On opposite sides of the fight, but constantly thrown together because of her.

"Awkward! Could be a novel..." The phone rang. Thank goodness, another person to talk to.

"Hey Bev." It was Sam, she had expected Hal.

"Hi Sam!" She hadn't heard from him since the day in the hospital. She had been slightly disappointed that he hadn't collected on his hero's reward.

"How are you?" She asked first.

"I'm good. How are you healing up?" The small talk was still necessary and for some reason that made her feel sad.

"I'm getting the hang of the crutches. My ankle is almost 100%. I think I'll go back to the office Monday. What's up?" She sensed that he hadn't called to chit-chat.

"Well, I almost didn't call, but I wanted you to hear it from me first," the silence was deafening.

"What?" She braced herself, had something happened to Hal, to Ethan, but then why would Sam know about anything that happened to Ethan?

"There's been another fire." He let it sink in and braced for the barrage of questions that he knew was coming.

She didn't let him down, "What? Where?"

"Another vacant building, this time south of the tracks, we had a fatality. It had been so long since the last fire that we hoped it was over."

"Are you sure it's arson? Who died?" She had not thought of the arson fires for at least a week herself.

"Off the record?" He was officer Gant now, she visualized him in the uniform and reflector glasses.

"Sure."

"Yes, same MO. Mac has arrested a man by the name of Warren, Oliver Warren. He's an ex-Vietnam vet whose been placed at two of the fires, basically homeless, kind of crazy. The gentleman that died was another homeless man, Rondo Martinez."

"That's terrible. Does Hal know?"

"He's being briefed. I thought I would give you a heads up."

"Thanks. I get the sense you still don't think Mac's on the right track."

"I don't know, something still doesn't add up. Oliver Warren's crazy, but he doesn't have a motive. Now it's a homicide. I just can't see pinning that on Warren."

They were both silent for a moment, processing it all.

"Hey Sam?" She felt a sudden need to cheer him up.

"Yeah?"

"How about hashing it out over dinner? You know I still owe you one," she smiled at the idea.

He paused before answering, but only for a moment, "You feel like getting out of the house, huh?"

"Well, sure!" She hadn't really thought about logistics, but it could be done.

"What about Hal?" He asked. She felt a bit guilty, she hadn't really thought about Hal when she offered.

"What about Hal?" She retorted. "Sounds like he's going to be busy tonight with the new lead story."

"Ok. I'll come by around seven," he was all business.

"Ok, see you in a while."

She hurried to her best ability to get cleaned up on one foot, looking forward to the evening.

"Arson and homicide. Now that's a story," she nodded, agreeing with herself.

16

Jacob Murray waited in the soon to be foyer of The Belle Hotel. He had chosen the name after reading an article in the local paper about the Lauren Belle, a paddle boat on the Mississippi. It sounded so international and meant beautiful. The hotel was going to be beautiful, maybe the most beautiful thing ever, except for Netty Bingham.

She was like a perfectly chiseled ice sculpture, blonde tresses, the sky in her eyes, cream colored skin. He had been thinking more and more about what cool delights were hidden under those elaborate skirts and how he might melt them. Janine still refused to see him, just as well, he needed to move on to someone of his own social standing.

Netty appeared in the door frame as if his very thinking of her made her materialize. She looked lovely in a low cut tight bodice of light blue, full skirt flowing. A perfect picture.

"Oh, Miss Bingham. Thank you for coming. I have had you on my mind."

She smiled and offered him her hand, which he kissed affectionately.

"Of course Mr. Murray. Your note said it was urgent. Is there something wrong with the Belle?" They had both taken to referring to the hotel as if it were a living entity.

"No, no, nothing like that. Something pleasant, I hope, for both of us," he took her other hand.

"Miss Bingham...Netty...I have something I want to discuss with you."

She looked directly into his eyes with those deep blue pools, her bosom was enhanced by her dress, she was intoxicating.

"Yes," she paused, "Jacob."

If she anticipated that he was about to propose she didn't let on. He was certain she felt affectionate towards him, she needed him, of that he was sure. He continued.

"It has been nothing but a pleasure working with you on the Belle. You are the driving force for me to finish. You are helping me become the man I want to be."

She smiled, but didn't comment.

"What I am going to ask may surprise you, I hope not. I hope you have seen this future for yourself....I want you to help me run the Belle not only as a business partner, but as my partner in life."

Her face changed a bit, perhaps surprise, but from what he could tell she wasn't offended.

"Why Mr. Murray...Jacob," she was a bit taken back but not for long. "I cannot lie, I have thought about you in deeper ways than a business partner–" He cut her off.

"Then marry me, be my wife Netty Bingham."

He would have bedded her on the spot, but protocol must be followed, at least for now.

Netty's mind was whirling. Marriage had crossed her

mind as an option to her plan, but she had dismissed it knowing Jacob Murray's weakness for women. She had never dreamed he would take action this soon. She had been courting Clint through correspondence and his occasional visits to town. She expected a proposal from him in due time.This would take some thought.

"This is rather sudden Mr. Murray...there is so much to consider," she turned away, she could tell this was not the answer he wanted.

"We are an unstoppable team, Netty. Your beauty, my know how in business. We both love the Belle already. And I have come to love you, Miss Bingham," he pulled her to him.

She looked up into his handsome face, those long lashed eyes, and she let him kiss her.

"Please," he whispered in her ear as they embraced. She smiled over his shoulder.

"This will not be the last time you beg, Jacob Murray," she thought to herself.

She pulled away. Looking at him, hating him and wanting him at the same time.

"Yes. I will marry you, Jacob Murray, but I would ask you not to announce our engagement until the opening night of the Belle."

His eyes shone, "Of course! It will be the perfect evening for it. Oh my dear, we'll be wonderful together. I have something for you." He turned away to a work table and brought out a small velvet box, "Until such time as we make our intended marriage official will you wear this locket for me?" It was a pretty little gold locket on a gold chain.

"How lovely, Mr. Murray."

"May I?" He indicated for her to turn so he could put it on her neck. She lifted her hair and he latched it behind her then tenderly kissed the latch. The touch of his lips sent heat into Netty's icy heart and flushed her cheeks.

Jacob Murray smiled to himself. Netty Bingham was his.

They spent the better part of the next hour discussing plans for the opening night, their engagement party, and details for the hotel.

After kissing her secret fiancé goodbye and turning out the door, Netty Bingham smiled to herself. Jacob Murray was hers.

JACOB MURRAY'S new standing in the community as an entrepreneur and business owner had propelled him into the small town's political circle. He was asked to attend city meetings with the mayor, sheriff and other prominent businessmen.

Most of these meetings were not what Jacob would consider entertainment. Did these people really care about public hangings offending women or whether or not to serve Indians in the dry goods store? The only topic of late that interested him was the construction of the Belle. The sooner he got it finished and opened, the sooner he could have Netty completely. She had denied him any physical advances, Janine would not take him as a customer, and he was going wild with desire.

Tonight's topics of discussion were once again of little interest to him. He wanted to go back to the bar and find a willing playmate.

"There is just no other way around it..." The mayor was proposing a per-head fee on the cattle brought to town for water.

"It's done in other cattle crossings, I hear in Fort Worth

it's a dollar a head!" Nels Bloom, the owner of the lumber company, got a "Hear Hear!" from someone in the back of the room.

"Of course we have to do it," Jacob agreed. "If we don't we will have every cow and hand for 200 miles mudding our streets and fouling the water!" It didn't bother him in the least that his own brother would be directly affected, quite the contrary, he enjoyed the thought.

The mayor nodded, "Let's put it to a vote then. All in favor say 'Aye'." The "Aye's" were called from around the room. "All against signify by the raising of hands." There was no one in the room opposed. "Very well. Let the city ordinance stand by a unanimous vote of its representative town's people. The sheriff will impose a two cent per animal charge for ranchers bringing their cattle through town to use the stock tanks or the Sand River within town limits."

The secretary wrote furiously. By the end of the week the ordinance was signed and posted throughout town and near the necessary waterways. It wasn't long before the news, and the trouble it caused, spread through the region.

17

———

Bev had been living in sweat pants and eating Ben and Jerry's for two weeks and her wardrobe was limited not only by the cast on her leg, but also by the ten pounds she'd gained. A silk T-shirt and knee length skirt was all she could find to fit her perilous shape.

"Where to?' Sam asked after he had worked her into the car.

"Somewhere they serve salad!" She had to start somewhere.

He suggested a family restaurant in Marfa that had a fairly broad menu. She agreed.

During the 30-minute drive she could feel a distance between them, even in the small car.

"Any new news on the fire?" She felt certain he would be into the subject.

"No, not really. I'm at a loss," he became silent again. She decided to try another subject.

"I've been working on the historical piece I told you about, like a month ago." She couldn't tell if he was really listening but she continued, "evidently there was a love triangle between two brothers and a beautiful hotel owner."

"Hmm."

She knew he wasn't listening now, so she kept going.

"Yes, she was screwing them both and they had no clue…" she waited.

"What?" He finally tuned back in.

"Ha ha, gotcha," she grinned and he chuckled.

"Sounds like the kind of thing novels are made of."

"That's what I thought, what I don't get is what she wanted with two of them. One man is plenty."

"Probably depends on the man, some are more than plenty!" He grinned from ear to ear now.

"You're terrible. Cute, but terrible."

She backhanded him playfully on the shoulder. Somehow since he had found her on the cliff edge the animosity she had first felt for him had changed. She liked the friendly banter and she liked him.

Dinner was good. There was salad, which was great, and a bottle of wine, which was excellent. He told her what he knew about the fires of 1881, she told him about her Dad. Sam relaxed after his meal and his second glass of wine, but he still looked distracted.

"It must be demanding being a cop," she offered her sympathy.

"Yeah, demanding, but rewarding too. I see a lot of shit; drugs, destruction, degradation, but there are those moments when it's all worth it. You live for those moments." He stopped and caught her gaze.

She held it, "Tell me some of them." He had a knack for disarming her. Her heart was pounding.

"Oh you know…passing out speeding tickets to tourists, helping a gal with a broke down car or rescuing a local journalist from a cliff ledge." His grin was warm and wicked at the same time. They had both leaned closer to one another, magnetically drawn.

"Funny," she whispered. She had his full attention now. She recognized a look in his eyes, desire, longing. She could feel herself giving in.

"I thought so," he raised his eyebrows and she melted, his eyes twinkled.

"Let's get out of here." Even as he was saying it she was already gathering her purse and medical equipment.

"Sexy," she thought as she wobbled and hopped out the door.

They made it to the car. He turned her to himself and steadied her against the door frame. He was so warm, so genuine, he smelled fantastic. He stroked Bev's face, studying her.

"Sam," she whispered. Before she could stop him, he kissed her softly, holding back a flood of passion. She rose up to him and kissed him back with more gusto than she had intended.

He took in an audible breath and the floodgate began to crack.

"God, what am I doing?" She thought to herself and then he put both hands around her face kissing her again and it didn't matter. Never had she felt like this, wanted like this.

He suddenly stopped, "I'm too drunk to drive, professional courtesy you know, follow me." He took her hand and then chuckled and scooped her up, "Allow me."

There was a small park behind the courthouse across the street. It was shadowed and grassy. He lay down beside her where they could see the stars.

"I wouldn't have pegged you for an exhibitionist, aren't we breaking some law?" She teased.

"I won't tell if you don't." He shrugged, "I'm a public servant, I do a lot of things in public." It was his turn to kiss her, hard this time, she felt wonderfully dizzy. He was solid, every muscle tightly wound. She closed her eyes and breathed in the smell of the night, the grass, his skin. His hands and mouth were hot, setting fire everywhere they touched. How convenient her skirt choice had been.

He paused just once, those beautiful grey eyes beaming, asking her permission. She answered by pulling his face to hers and they both laughed. Neither one of them noticed the inconvenience of her cast.

SAM HAD RELUCTANTLY LEFT her bed early in the morning. As day dawned and Bev's head cleared she began to flirt with regret and then she would remember those eyes twinkling like the stars above his head and she would be lost again.

"Sam?" Who would have guessed it. They had started off as professional combatants. Although, she had to admit that she had always liked a good fight. Still there was Hal, he had been there for her, he was her boss and she owed him something. Didn't she?

The phone rang.

"Hello?"

"Hey baby!" Hal sounded intoxicated or maybe just very excited.

"Hi, Hal," she tried to match his enthusiasm.

"Have you heard? Of course you have! You're a journalist!" She was lost for a moment.

"Oh, yes, the fire. I heard there was a homicide this time." She played with her yogurt, subconsciously wondering why he hadn't told her yesterday.

"Yeah, great headliner huh?!" Morose but true, she thought.

"Send me the facts and I'll get to work on it." She could focus for a lead story. This had to be a "barn burner" in his book.

"Sorry Darlin'," he put on his best Texas drawl, "I got this one. Not many of these type of stories in this town."

"Well, crap," she thought, "what a glory hound."

"I could do the legwork," she was trying to be cute but only sounding desperate.

"Ha ha ha! Funny! Legwork, I get it. Nah, I got it under control. It is my paper after all."

"Well, Ok. I thought I would come in to the office Monday."

His comment made her feel like maybe she had been gone too long, that there was not going to be any need for her if she stayed away much longer.

"I'll finish up my work here this afternoon and I'll come by."

She was about to tell him not to, but thought it might be a good time to set him straight on their relationship.

"Ok," she really didn't want the drama, but he was too wired to notice the defeat in her voice.

"I'll bring Ben and Jerry's!" She was about to say no, that she didn't need any more, but he had already hung up the phone.

"Great, two men!" She picked up the vintage picture from the table and studied the blonde again. What would *she* say to her unwanted suitor?

18

———

In the fall of 1881, the already desiccated land of southwest Texas was withering under an eleven month drought. Water holes and feeder creeks that had served ranches for the last twenty years were gone. Ranchers, desperate to save years of their family's livelihood, raided local town's water supplies. Most tried by dark of night, often revealed by the very animals they hoped to save. Confrontations between lawmen and ranchers ended in confiscation of livestock, jail time, and sometimes worse. The ranchers were at a distinct disadvantage to organize a collective dispute due to sheer distances between them. But despite the difficulties, several land owners in the region managed to meet, put their demands to paper and authorize Clint Murray as their spokesman.

Clint, demands in hand, left the Murray ranch with three of his wranglers and drove 100 thirsty head of cattle into town to give their demands impact.

Clint spent the evening ride contemplating the possible outcomes of this showdown. The town leaders could relent, understand the rancher's plight and work with them, unlikely. The sheriff and posse would meet them at the river and arrest them, jail them and fine them all, very likely. Or they would be met with gunfire and possibly die fighting for water, the least appealing and, luckily, the least likely. It all made him weary.

He had nearly lost all interest in the affairs of the ranch. Clint couldn't keep his mind on any task at all since meeting and corresponding with Netty. He had only met her twice, but had exchanged letters with her almost daily for the last four months. She was gentile, intelligent and beautiful. More than he could have ever hoped to find in a lifelong companion. He had never thought about a future or a family until his father's death and meeting Miss Bingham. He hoped he could convince her that he would be a faithful and loving husband, father and provider.

After this stand with the town was finally cleared up he would ask for her hand. The thought lightened his mood as he plodded behind the scrawny cattle. Money would be tight on the ranch this year after Jacob taking his share and the drought taking its toll on the herd. Damn his brother and damn the blasted watering fees. Clint set his jaw and tried to think more pleasant thoughts of his possible future with Netty Bingham.

It wasn't long before the ragged shadows of the tops of the cotton wood trees became a clearer silhouette in the night sky as the herd headed down into the river valley. The sheriff and the mayor were there to meet them at the bank of the Sand Creek Crossing, just as Clint had predicted. The thirsty cattle, enticed by the smell of the creek, began to press forward, not to be denied relief by six men on horseback.

"Who goes there?" The sheriff was ready, loaded

shotgun resting across his lap, his six-shooters strapped to his waist.

"Clint Murray, Sheriff. We've come to water our herd."

The ranch hands struggled to keep the cattle from moving forward, they wouldn't wait much longer.

"You know we can't let you do that without payment, Mr. Murray," The Mayor was emboldened by his armed compadre.

"I've also brought demands from the ranchers of the area, we would like to officially oppose the per head fee."

Clint's horse began to fidget under him, feeling the tension both between the men and in the herd.

"Señor!" Clint's man, Miguel, warned him just in time. He pulled up his horse spinning around as the lead steer broke through the standoff. The rest of the cattle blindly followed. There was bellowing of men and beasts, Clint shouted his demands, the sheriff taking them as threats. Shots were fired. When the dust cleared, the cattle were headlong in the creek drinking deeply, one of the ranch hands had been killed and Clint Murray and his remaining men were jailed overnight.

The next morning he was forced to pay a $20 fine before he and his cattle were released. Little good his stand had made. He couldn't disguise his frustration and anger when he went to meet Netty Bingham on the boardwalk of Main Street the next day.

"Mr. Murray! Are you all right?" Netty had heard of his recent misfortune of course and no doubt so had his brother. This added salt to an already chaffed and wounded pride.

"I'm fine. Miss Bingham. A bruised ego perhaps. I am better for seeing you. You look wonderful." These past months of correspondence had made him feel closer to Netty than anyone he had ever known.

"Will you appeal your cause with the mayor?" Despite her vengeful heart she came across genuinely concerned for his being wronged.

"I've already tried. They refused our demands. I don't know what will happen when the other ranchers find out. I fear for the safety of the town, and for you Miss Bingham."

He didn't seem to have any fight left in him that she could see, which made her despise him more. They stopped under a tired tree and tried to use the weak shade it provided. He held her elbow and kept her from walking on.

"Miss Bingham, I don't get to see you often, but I feel as though our letters have brought us closer together."

She waited, looking up at him, doe eyed, knowing what was coming this time.

"Netty, if I may be so bold, I have come to love you through our letters and I would like to ask you something," he was nervous.

She pretended to be charmed, "Yes, Mr. Murray?"

"Would you consider coming to the ranch and..." he took a deep breath, "and being my wife?"

She smiled, not the kind smile of a lover but the vicious smile of a vixen. Clint Murray was too enamored to see the difference.

"Mr. Murray...Clint," she whispered for effect. "I have come to care for you as well these past months," she took his rough, weathered hands.

"The ranch will provide for us for many years, and any children that may come along," he blushed slightly as he said it, a desperate fool for her affection.

"You have given me a lot to consider," she could barely stand to look at his sad, worn face. "I've started to build a life for myself in town with the hotel. It would be quite a change from what I thought would be my future."

His countenance fell further yet. He looked sick, like she had kicked him.

"Will you allow me a few days to consider your offer?"

He didn't want to, but he had no choice, "Of course. I'll be here through the week."

She thanked him by reaching up and kissing his cheek. He flushed and they continued on their walk.

"Will you do me one more favor while you're here?" She had hooked him now. He would do anything for her.

"Of course, anything."

"Will you escort me to the grand opening party of the Belle this Friday? I don't want to attend on my own. I will be able to give you your answer then." He nodded, knowing full well that Jacob would be there.

"Won't Jacob want to escort you?" The question actually caught her slightly off guard, but only for a moment.

"Of course he will be there, but we are business associates and he will be very busy being a good host. If it bothers you to be there with him, I understand." She pleaded with her lying eyes.

"No, no it's no trouble. I've dealt with my brother my whole life. I would be honored to escort you."

She smiled at him and took his arm. She had set the stage for the final act.

Jacob Murray drew in deeply on his cigar and admired the hotel lobby. The renovations where spectacular, everything was perfect for tonight's grand opening. True they had cost him almost everything he had, but it would be worth it to have what he always wanted; respect, money and freedom. It was already worth it. He would finally get to announce he and Netty's engagement and finally get to undress that cool, slender body. He shivered just thinking of it.

The front door opened quietly, he half expected it to be her when he turned around, but to his surprise it was Janine.

He leaned on the counter, "We're closed until tonight."

Janine wasn't deterred by his cold reception.,"I thought you might give me a private tour." She made her way to him and leaned on the counter, taking off her wrap.

She was powdered and painted perfectly, hair swept up off her long neck. She had the locket on that he had given her. He reached over and fingered the locket between her breasts. She smiled and let him.

"I've missed you," she said.

"You have a strange way of showing it." He busied himself putting his cigar out.

"The hotel is stunning," she pretended to look around, watching him.

"Mmhmm." She was stunning. He came around the counter to where she stood.

"Well," she acted as if she were about to leave, "I guess I'll come back this evening."

He grabbed her by the back of her neck, turning her to him and violently kissing her, she feigned dislike, then smiled and kissed him back.

"Why Jacob! You have missed me too," she pressed up against him, he wanted everything she was offering.

"A tour." He undressed her with his eyes, "Come with me."

He showed her one of the beautifully appointed rooms, pushing her in the door and slamming it behind them.

They spent the afternoon breaking in the new feather mattress and re-igniting their affair. There was no denying the heat between them. He needed her and wanted Netty at the same time. As far as Jacob was concerned there was no reason he couldn't have both.

Janine and Jacob were saying their sorted goodbyes in the lobby when Netty walked into the hotel. She stopped short at the sight of them together.

"Miss Bingham," Janine smiled knowingly, "Mr. Murray was just showing me your beautiful hotel. Tonight's grand opening is the talk of the town."

Jacob leaned against the counter watching the two women.

"Thank you, Janine is it?" Netty removed her hat and wrap, "Will you be attending?"

"I wouldn't miss it for anything," Janine headed to the door.

"Until tonight then," Netty let her pass, noticing the simple gold locket around her neck.

She turned to Jacob after she left.

"Darling!" He came to her and embraced her, she could smell Janine on his skin, her stomach turned, "Tonight! It's finally here!"

She disguised her disdain as passion in her kiss.

"Yes, tonight," she thought.

19

———

Bev spent the day piddling around her tiny studio. She tried to read and then tried to write, but couldn't focus on either one. She rehearsed in her mind what she was going to tell Hal when he showed up. She liked him, respected him personally and professionally, but just didn't think there was any romantic future for them. She knew he wouldn't like it, but she didn't foresee any real confrontation. After all, he was an intelligent man.

She still questioned if she was doing the right thing, not with Hal, she knew that had to end, but with Officer Gant. What was she doing with Sam? There was last night but did that mean there was anything else? He had infuriated her most of the time, but as she had gotten to know him she was drawn to his genuine strength and kindness. It didn't hurt that he was easy on the eyes.

Could she honestly see him as an intellectual equal, a life partner, or just a hunk in a uniform? Maybe she was over thinking all this. It was one night, he hadn't even called her today. What did that mean?

Hal would be here in a while. She cleaned up the

kitchen and brushed her hair. She put on some music and sat down at the computer. Her mind began to wander.

What exactly did these arson fires have in common? The buildings were abandoned, except for the last one, which was more than likely a fluke. So the person setting the fires had to know they were empty, be familiar with the town. A local, like Sam suspected.

Two of the fires had been set during the summer months when teenagers would be their most mischievous, but two had been set in the fall when school was in session. Most criminal mischief slowed when the weather cooled and school began, kids were too busy or too tired. So, more than likely, an adult.

All four fires had been set with the accelerant acetone. The only thing Bev had ever used acetone for was nail polish remover. A rogue salon operator or nail tech, maybe gone crazy from the fumes? Ha. She typed "acetone" into the search on her computer.

*"**Acetone** (systematically named ***propanone**) is the organic compound with identified the formula (CH3)2CO. It is the simples ketone. A colorless, mobile, flammable liquid.*

Acetone is miscible with water, H2O, and serves as an important solvent, typically as the solvent of choice for cleaning purposes in a laboratory. About 6.7 million tons of acetone were produced worldwide in 2010, for use as a solvent and also in production of methyl methacrylate and biphenyl A. Used commonly as a building building block in organic chemistry. Familiar household uses of acetone are as the active ingredient in nail polish remover and as paint thinner.

Common uses; industrial solvent and cleaner, stain and paint thinner, in health and beauty products. Used in laboratories to clean lab equipment, as well as to clean fiberglass, porcelain and glass. Can be used to transfer and remove ink."

I⊤ WAS PRETTY COMMON, could be used in lots of places. Maybe the science lab at the school or a janitorial supply company would be a good start. Could they trace particular batches of the chemical she wondered? Did Alpine police even have access to forensic science? Too bad these things couldn't be done like they were on TV. The case would have been solved in 30 minutes. She would share her thoughts with Sam when she saw him next.

She wondered when that would be. He still hadn't called. She wondered what he had thought of their date. Maybe she should call him. No, that would be obsessive and look desperate. Now she remembered why she didn't do relationships well. She was always second guessing, questioning herself and her lover's intentions.

"Beverly, calm down you're always getting so worked up." She could hear her dad's voice in her head as if it were yesterday, "Take deep breaths."

They had been standing in the foyer of the little church, he was in his finest suit and she in the chosen white dress. She had started to hyperventilate just as they began to enter the sanctuary and walk down the aisle. For several awkward moments she had to sit down and put her head between her knees. He had reassured her. Poor Ethan had waited at the altar wondering if she had changed her mind. But she had pulled herself together, taken her father's arm and pushed through her anxiety, marrying Ethan.

Their three-year marriage had been wrought with frustration. He had assumed things of her and she had demanded things of him. In the end it was a lack of common courtesy for one another's feelings that built an impenetrable wall between them, offense by offense. They simply stopped caring if they hurt each other or not. If they could lose respect for one another that quickly how could they have really ever been in love? In both their minds getting married had been a mistake and they agreed to end it.

She wanted to be sure never to repeat that mistake again. It was too painful, painful to fail, painful to be so misled by someone, and painful to admit to being misleading herself. Whatever this was with officer Gant, she had to take care. She had to be honest with him and herself.

She heard a car drive up. It was Hal with his ice cream. Oh how she dreaded letting him down or hurting his feelings, but honesty was, after all, her new policy when it came to relationships. He came bounding in from the van and enveloped her with his long arms.

"Hi Babe!" He kissed her then untangled himself and sat down in the tiny kitchen with two spoons and his ice cream. She reluctantly joined him.

"Hal, we need to talk," she tried after they had a couple of bites.

"Can you believe it? A fourth fire!" His dark eyes shown with excitement. Great, she thought, he's still on some headline high.

"Did you get your story written?" She dutifully asked.

"Most of it – I can't stay long. I want to wrap it up tonight, but I had to see you." His focus changed and he looked at her adoringly.

"Now or never," thought Bev.

"Hal, I need to talk to you." She took his hand. He misread her intention and leaped up and kissed her.

"Hal, wait! Stop!" She literally had to push him back in his chair. He was deterred but only for a moment. He smiled.

"Sorry honey, you're just so irresistible."

"This may be harder than I thought. Short and sweet Connors, like removing a Band-Aid," she thought. She stood up to better fend him off before she proceeded.

"Hal, I think we better stop seeing each other," there, she had said it.

Hal was still smiling, either he hadn't heard her or was refusing to listen.

"What do you mean? We're great together," he dismissed her comment and turned his attention back to the ice cream.

"Yes, Hal, I think we're a good team, professionally. And we are certainly great friends with lots in common. I just don't think we should be romantically involved." She waited.

His spoon hung in front of his mouth and a furrow crossed his brow. He stopped eating and slowly stood up, finally comprehending what she was saying.

"You want to break up?" He said slowly.

"Yes, Hal." She felt awful.

"Wow. Didn't see that one coming." He ran his long fingers through his hair. His tall body slumped, "I thought we had something." As usual he looked like a crane, but now he looked like a really sad crane.

"I'm sorry. I didn't want to hurt you. I thought we could have something too, but I just don't feel that way about you Hal."

He came over to her, "Are you sure?" He cocked his head sideways.

She nodded and avoided his gaze. Before she knew what

was coming he had embraced her and was kissing her passionately.

"Hal," she squirmed and used her crutch to wedge them apart, "I'm sure."

He backed off, "It's not because I'm your boss is it? Because that is no big deal for me."

"No, that isn't it," although she hadn't fully contemplated how this break up was going to affect her job.

He nodded, "Ok then." He spoke softly, his long narrow face looking even longer, "I guess I'll see you at work."

"Yes, I'll be in Monday. Let me know if you need me to work on anything before that."

He nodded again. And headed to the door. He didn't say anything else as he stooped through the door frame and got in his van.

They were both too involved in the moment to notice Sam Gant's patrol car just leaving the parking lot. Sam had seen Hal's last attempted persuasion of Bev through her window.

Unfortunately, he had not stayed long enough to see Bev turn Hal down.

THE OFFICE WAS UNUSUALLY QUIET. Elena was MIA, not unusual, but the phone was quiet too, as was the press room. Was it a holiday that she had forgotten about? Her office seemed drab and she was completely uninspired with the current list of leads that had been left on her desk. Perhaps it was her mood in general.

She had waited all weekend for Sam to call. No call. She hadn't pegged him as a "one night stand" kind of guy. He could not have looked at her the way he had without feeling something for her, she was certain, maybe. She decided if she didn't hear from him today she was going to swallow her pride and call him, find out what the problem was. She hated leaving things unfinished. It wasn't in her nature.

No one had brought her any coffee this morning, the first of many side effects to the "breakup" she was sure. She set off to find the coffee maker in the office kitchen, surely there was a break room somewhere. She felt foolish that she hadn't been here long enough to know. Not finding anything resembling a kitchen in the front, she went through the press room doors. The press was still and silent, like a sleeping giant, waiting to be roused at the next great story. There was a glass front office on the other side of the large room that looked promising.

Within the glassed offices she found a small room with a counter and sink and a very old coffee pot. The last person that had attempted to make coffee had left it to burn on the bottom of the glass pot, leaving a very unappetizing dark brown glaze.

It would be easier to go buy some down the street if she wasn't on crutches. But she was here and on a mission. She found the coffee and the filters in the cabinet above. Maybe there would be something to scrub the pot out under the sink, nothing. There were several other large cabinets in the room, maybe one had cleaning supplies. First one had miscellaneous office supplies, paper, pens and other obsolete items from the pre-computer age. The second appeared to have equipment, tools, and parts for the press. There was replacement cartridges and cleaner. Finally in the last cabinet was common cleaning supplies and a scrubbing sponge.

She was busy at her task, so when Raul, came around the corner she jumped.

"Sorry, Miss Connors," he grinned cunningly. "Can I help?"

"My God, Raul! We are now even!" She smiled back, but didn't like the vibe she was getting. "No, I finally found everything I needed. Want some coffee?"

"No, ma'am. I don't drink it." He eyed the cabinets. She was obviously tramping in his territory.

"I'll be out of here in a minute. Is there any creamer anywhere?" He went directly a cabinet and pulled some out.

"Thanks," she quickly finished her pouring and mixing and left him guarding his turf.

"No problem," he watched her until she exited the press room.

"Man this town has some characters." She took a sip of the extra strong brew and decided not to wait any longer to call Gant.

His recording came on immediately. "Hmm, not taking calls or not taking *my* calls," she wondered.

"Hey Sam!" She tried not to sound too anxious. "Just wanted you to know that I was thinking of you." She paused, what to say next? "I thought, um, well, that I would have heard from you by now. I know you're a busy public servant and all...anyway, you know where to find me. Have a great day!" Pathetic, she thought as she hung up.

"You busy?" She jumped out of her skin for the second time in an hour!

Hal stood in the doorway, hands on the door casing above him like he was going to do chin ups.

"Not yet, I just got my coffee."

He looked sad or concerned, she couldn't tell.

"I didn't even know we had a coffee pot." He came in and sat down. "I just wanted to let you know that our personal relationship, or lack thereof," he smiled weakly, "won't interfere with our professional relationship. No hard feelings and all that." He didn't sound very convincing but the wounds were new after all.

"Thank you, I appreciate that," she offered.

"And to show that I'm serious, I'd like to have you to my place for dinner." She started to refuse but he held up his long hand and shook his head. "To discuss these arson fires. I need you to rework some of the copy for a feature in our 'year-end events' issue."

She wanted to write the piece but didn't trust his motives. He could tell.

"Bring Gant if you want."

Gant? How long had he been standing in the doorway, did he hear her whole phone message?

She took a deep breath, "Umm, I appreciate your honesty Hal. You know that I would love to help you on the arson piece." She hesitated again.

"I make a mean homemade ravioli!" He smiled and seemed his usual self, pretending to pout when she hesitated again.

"Ok. When?" She was certain she had just made a mistake.

He clapped his hands. "Great! How about Thursday?"

"Ok, Thursday it is."

20

Netty put great care into her evening outfit and personal care. Every hair and ruffle would be in place for this extraordinary event. She smiled at herself in the mirror as she thought about cutting one Murray down at the knee with the help of the other. Perhaps they would even come to blows or shoot one another. How fitting. Regardless, she would enjoy every moment of breaking Clint's heart, like he broke hers. If Jacob lived through the evening, he would be next.

She thought for a moment about her beloved Jace. Her cheeks flushed with anger and sorrow but she would not allow herself to cry and ruin her powder.

"Take it and go, Netty," his voice whispered.

She closed her eyes and saw his blonde mop hair and blue eyes, toddler legs running to her when he was a child, embracing her. He had been the only one who had ever cared about her, now she had to take care of herself. And she intended to do just that.

Janine would have to go too. As much as she despised Jacob Murray for the death of her brother, he was her mouse to play with in this cat's game, not Janine's. She couldn't bear to be second to Janine when it came to Jacob's needs.

All that would change soon. They would be married as agreed by the end of the week and he would need only her.

She pinched her cheeks and smoothed the front of her dress. Perfect. Neither Clint nor Jacob would know what hit them.

THE HOTEL ENTRANCE doors were open wide inviting in the awe inspired guests. The gas lit crystal chandelier cast its light on the gold and ruby velvet papered walls and the deep carved rug on the warm oak hardwood floor. The grand staircase curved gracefully down and around the hand carved front desk. Netty had insisted on the beautiful silver and mahogany inlaid cash register made by the same company that made the scale in the assayer's office. There were fine oil paintings in ornate frames hanging from wires along the grand hallway that led to the grand dining hall and ballroom.

Eight luxurious guest rooms were on the second floor each with their own bathing tub and water closet. The Belle was one of the first hotels in the region with indoor facilities, adding to its opulence. The four remaining rooms were on the first floor and shared one bathing room. Large ferns on marble stands and gilded framed mirrors decorated the dining/ball room. It could seat 150 people and the ceilings were sixteen feet high. Three more gas lit crystal chandeliers hung from the center of the room. All in all, the Belle was a gem glittering in the desert.

Netty had already taken up residence in the owner's

suite so she could be on hand for the finishing work on the hotel and for the final preparations of tonight's event. After their wedding Jacob would be coming to live with her. They had planned the four-room residence together. Both enjoying the finer things they had never been able to secure in their previous lives and couldn't do without in this one. She glided through the apartment feeling like a princess.

"Soon it will all be mine," she said out loud as she closed the solid door and headed to the stairs.

The entryway lighting glowed thick and warm through the dusty air so characteristic of this country. Fashioned guests were milling about admiring the lobby and its appointments. The color of the scene suggested a water-color painting, everything a bit hazy at the edges. The night was warm despite the season and the scent of overdressed men and over powdered women rose to the landing where Netty stood. She waited for a moment, looking for either of her intended suitors. Seeing neither she made her entrance to greet her guests.

Her association with the hotel and with Jacob had given her some elevation in the community, but the women in town were suspicious of her beauty and the men were jealous of her good fortune in business.

She had no friends here.

Just as well, she didn't want any. All she wanted was justice for the death of her brother and, in the process. to win this wonderful hotel and the lifestyle it would afford. She wanted neither Jacob nor Clint beyond their usefulness to her to reach these goals. Her thoughts were swirling with the evening's possibilities as she expertly smiled and welcomed the couples in the room.

Clint caught her eye standing in the doorway holding his hat. He looked overwhelmed, prematurely defeated. She knew what he was thinking, and he was right. How could he compete with this? She went to him quickly, to falsely reassure him before he ran away. She wanted him here for her own purposes. Without him, revenge wouldn't be as sweet.

"Oh, Clint," she greeted him more enthusiastically and familiarly than he had expected. She could tell he was momentarily relieved. "I'm so glad you're here," she continued to gush, taking his arm and leading him into the room. "Can I offer you something to drink? Take your hat?" He looked around nervously.

"Looking for Jacob," she thought.

"A whiskey will do."

He surprised her, she wouldn't have thought him a drinker. He was nervous. It made the ink in her black heart pump wildly. She poured him a double. A drunk Clint was more likely to do rash things in anger.

Clint slammed the amber liquid back and handed the glass back, she filled it again. In a few moments the alcohol eased the tension in his face and shoulders.

"You look beautiful tonight." He looked at her for the first time since he came in.

"Thank you, Clint. How do you like the finished product?" She indicated the room.

He glanced around, really seeing the room for the first time as well.

"It's beautiful. I'm glad my family's money was spent on quality at least. You're doing, I'm sure. My brother has no taste." He finished the second drink and boldly poured himself another. She bristled at the comment, not in defense of Jacob, but because Jacob favored her and it stung her pride.

"Mr. Murray has delighted in every detail. He has been very good to me, Clint. Is there any way you could put your feelings aside for just this one night, it would mean so much to me." She touched his arm, pleaded with her eyes, encouraged with her stance.

He rose to his full height over her, emboldened by the drink. She would keep stirring his feelings, he would be wild with desire, betrayal and bitterness just when she needed his reaction the most.

He gazed at her and sighed, "For you I'll do anything."

"You are such a wonderful, thoughtful man, Clint. Come, let me show you the hotel."

He blindly followed her, drink in hand.

21

———

Monday came and went. Beverly checked her phone no less than 200 times, checking the connection, the batteries, and the ring volume. Sam didn't call, leave a message or even text so much as a "hey". She drove home to her tiny dumpy rooms confused, disillusioned and generally pissed off. She slammed the door of her car shut, wrangling her purse, computer and crutches.

"I am disavowing men!" She shouted to no one, as usual. She stopped at the door and pulled her mail out of the tin box at the entry, jamming the envelopes in her mouth. Once in, she spit them on the table. She stripped herself of her baggage and clothing, started her bath water and poured a glass of wine. She would sooth her wounded soul with water and wine. She glanced at the bills on the table, one envelope stood out. It was from the Jeff Davis County DMV. Maybe some good news about the ticket, she hoped.

She turned it over to open it and was startled to find a hand written note on the back of the envelope.

"You're welcome!" Was written in clean masculine hand,

vaguely familiar, from a recent citation, maybe? She tore it open steaming before she even read the computer generated form letter.

Mrs. Beverly Connors,
This letter is in regard to the recent motor vehicle citation #244589000045 registered to you under TXDL# 05156322. This citation has been cleared by the Department of Motor Vehicles in Jeff Davis County. There is no further action required on your part for this traffic violation.
Sincerely,
Tom Brady - County Clerk
Jeff Davis County
Fort Davis Texas

"THAT SON OF A BITCH." She crumbled the letter and threw it across the room. She had obviously been "PAID IN FULL" for the other night's services. She could almost hear him chuckling. She chugged the contents of her glass, then threw the glass.

"That arrogant prick! How could he, a cop no less!" More importantly, how could she have been so easily fooled, fallen so quickly?

"Shit, shit, shit!" She screamed jumping around the room on one good foot, forgetting she was naked. She steadied herself at the sink and drank directly out of the bottle. When her heart slowed she heard the water and had to scrambled to the bathroom to turn it off.

She plopped on the toilet with a slap of skin to porcelain.

"You fool, Beverly," she chided herself.

She sat there, bottle in hand, eyes closed, giving herself a mental thrashing. Why didn't she listen to her inner voice? Hadn't she felt uneasy about him from the beginning? She pondered long enough to drink a third of her bottle and for the bath water to cool. She cursed again, drained the tub part way and put in more hot water. She finally got in, sinking down under the water until she couldn't hold her breath anymore.

"Never again," she stated when she came up for air.

Never again did she want to be vulnerable, never again did she want to feel more than she should, never again did she want a man messing with her mind or her body. Most importantly, she would never let him know that he had gotten to her.

She took a deep breath, took a long drink and let the water and the wine lap at her inside and out. When she could muster the self-respect to get out of the tub, she got dressed in her sweats, cleaned up her mess and sat down at the kitchen table with her computer.

She typed furiously into the night, channeling her energy into the pages in front of her. The story of the Murray brothers flowed easily. It was easy to write of betrayal, disappointment and defeat. She felt a new found kinship with the beautiful, straight-laced woman with icy resolve in the tin-type photo.

22

It was difficult to find experienced musicians in this part of the country. Outside of the preacher's wife and the piano player in the bar, the choices were few. Jacob was determined to present his hotel as a high brow establishment, classical music was a must. He had paid for an upright piano and paid Miles Sanders, the saloon's piano man, to learn three new classical pieces.

Jacob listened from the hall just outside the dining–ball room. Miles was butchering the music, luckily the guests were either not paying attention or didn't know the difference, Jacob guessed the latter. It didn't matter, these people were not his real customers, they would come in time. Real elites with real money who knew fine music when they heard it. He made a mental note to find a real classical musician, maybe two.

The people were steadily making their way to the main hall for the food, somehow drawn by the tinny music. Jacob greeted them all as if they were the most important guests there, his job, to make this the most elegant night of their lives so word would spread. He had fretted so much about the details that he had almost forgotten the anticipated highlight of the evening, his announcement to marry Netty. For a moment his mind wandered to the after party he was looking forward to.

Unbeknownst to Netty, there were actually two parties. Jacob was planning on meeting Janine as well. Jacob's heart swelled with his selfish desires. He had it all. Everything he had ever wanted; the fine lifestyle, the praise and respect of men, and the bed of two women. He smiled wryly. "And not a shit head cow in sight," he thought.

He saw Netty turn the corner, a vision. At her side, Jacob couldn't believe it, his brother. Perhaps he had spoken too soon about cow shit. Netty had told him the story of Clint saving her from the Mexican, but that didn't ingratiate her to him for life, did it?

He forced his guile down with a shot of bourbon. He would take this opportunity to rub his brother's nose in his success. He walked up to them briskly. Extending his hand.

"Clint! I knew you couldn't stay away forever!" Clint took Jacob's hand dutifully, but didn't return his smile. Jacob ignored him and turned to Netty.

"My dear, you look stunning," he leaned over and kissed Netty on the cheek. Clint stiffened. Netty showed no indication of the excitement she was drawing from the tension between the two men. She smiled coyly addressing them both.

"I hope you don't mind, Mr. Murray, that I invited your brother. I was hoping you two could use tonight as new start and put your differences behind you." She had a hand on both men's arm, neither would concede to move away from her.

The brothers looked at each other. Bitterness swelled between them. Netty smiled inwardly.

A photographer who had traveled from El Paso rushed up, keeping the men from answering.

"A photo for the Sentinel, Mr. Murray?" Clint started to decline before he realized that the reporter was speaking to his brother.

"Of course, of course! Here in front of the ballroom!" He had Netty's elbow and escorted her into position. Jacob straightened his tie, straightened his vest and pocket watch, preening like a peacock.

"Come Clint," Netty pulled him to her other side. Jacob possessively put his arm around her waist, an action that didn't go unnoticed by Clint.

"One, Two, Three!" The photographer pushed the button on the camera, there was a flash of powder, the smell of sulfur and the three were held at that moment in that place for all of time.

Jacob quickly whisked Netty away feigning public relations responsibilities. Clint went sulking to the bar, with a promise from Netty that she would join him soon. He had no choice but to go and await his fate.

The proud parents of the Belle spent the evening pretentiously pointing out their darling's every feature to anyone one who would listen. It didn't matter what their guests thought, they were both lost in the perfection of their creation. They flitted and fawned. It did not matter that the first soup course was cold or that the dining hall got a bit stuffy. The hosts and the guests were more than pleased with the evening as it wore on.

After dinner, the tables were moved aside and an impromptu fiddle and piano serenaded the eager dancers. The tall windows were opened to let in the cooler night air. The whiskey, wine and beer continued to flow and the guests continued to have a wonderful time.

Netty, despite her better judgment, had accepted several glasses of wine during the evening as well as dances from several of the guests. It was at the finish of one of these rousing turns around the floor that she saw Clint standing at the edge of the room. Netty was brought back to her purposes and bowed out of the next dance to make her way to her suitor's side.

"We should dance, Clint!" She said to him, still flushed and breathless from the earlier exertion.

"Netty. I cannot stay much longer. I was hoping to have a word with you in private before I left," his tone was cool, all business.

"Think, Netty..." she forced herself to focus. She had to keep him here until Jacob made his announcement.

"Certainly, my dear," she pandered. She pressed her chest to the back of his arm as she took his lead to the front of the hotel. Her eyes darted around the room hoping to find the other Murray.

They were just rounding the corner in the hall when the music in the ballroom stopped and a ring of a glass brought the room to order.

"If I might have your attention!" Jacob Murray's voice rang clearly over the happy din in the room, "Please, quiet everyone!" Netty stopped Clint and turned to go back.

"No, Netty. Let's go," Clint held her arm.

"He may need–" she tried to pull free but he held her, he was strong for a moment.

"If I could have Miss Netty Bingham up at the front with me?" Jacob was calling for her.

"Please, Clint, I have to go."

Something in Clint's face changed, he held her gaze and the softness she had always seen there slowly faded. As his look hardened, he slowly let go of her arm.

She straightened her gown and headed back to the ballroom. If Clint wasn't going to play his part then she would rewrite the script. She would still break his heart and ruin his brother, she would just have to be content with not seeing the former in person.

"Ahh... there she is...please darling join me here at the front," Jacob held his hand out and Netty joined her intended at the front of the ballroom.

"It has been a wonderful evening and both Miss Bingham and I would like to thank you all for coming out to see our wonderful Belle Hotel. We hope to be part of this town and help celebrate many events in all of your lives for many years to come." The crowd applauded, when they slowed Jacob continued, "As you know, Miss Bingham and I have worked very hard and very closely together these long months." Jacob turned from the crowd toward Netty taking her hands in his. "It was during those months that she and I found each other. And so to make a perfect evening more perfect, I would like to announce our intended marriage. We will run the Belle as husband and wife!" The guests cheered, Netty couldn't help but smile genuinely, perhaps the wine had dulled the darkness in her for a moment.

Congratulations were coming at them from all sides as well as thanks for the evening. The music started up again and some persistent party goers continued to dance. Netty glanced up just in time to see Clint standing in the hall door frame. His face was dark and burdened. She smiled selfishly letting her disdain for him show clearly, he did not look shocked or wounded, only determined when he turned and walked down the dark hall.

"The curtain closes on the first act," she thought and turned her attention to Jacob.

23

The GPS led the way up and around the "subdivision" that was located on the Davis Mountain Ridge just northwest of Alpine. From what Bev could tell in the early evening light, there were no homeowner association or subdivision standards for this neighborhood. "Off the grid" definitely was the word for it.

She was beginning to wonder why she was making such an effort. No amount of professional acclaim was worth fighting off Hal all evening. Then again, everything had lost its appeal the last few days. She had even considered going back to Denver but that idea depressed her most of all.

She had called Sam and left messages begging, threatening and cursing him. She had gone to the courthouse in Fort Davis and spoken to his good friend, Goth Girl, and to the Sheriff's office and spoken to Officer Mac in person.

"On assignment," was all he would offer.

The local firemen were extremely entertained by the thought that she was tracking him down and especially by the thought that he couldn't be found. She sped, she littered and she looked in all the regular places she had seen his patrol car, constantly checking her rear view mirror. Sam had fallen off the face of the earth and no one seemed at all worried about it. It was driving Bev mad constantly wondering if he was truly working or was he avoiding her? Either way she wanted to find out the truth.

"Journalist," she chided herself.

A set of reflective numbers tacked on a tall cedar shrub marked Hal's property. She sighed wearily then made her way down the long dirt drive. There was a greying cedar plank home at the end with indigenous plants and cactus for landscape. The windows were glowing warmly, his signature green van was parked at the door. She gathered her portfolio and computer and stepped out of the car.

"Hey Girl," Hal chimed from his front porch. Bev could smell the Italian seasonings and garlic wafting out the door. He smiled broadly. "I'm so glad you came! I made a feast!" He stepped aside shepherding her in.

"It smells fantastic," she began to unwrap and unload. The austerity of Hal's office life was not carried over into his personal life. His living area looked like a library had exploded. Books, folders and printed materials of all kinds were piled on every available surface including the floor. There was a sort of network of trails leading to and fro to different areas of the room. After the initial shock, and thoughts of having a hoarder's intervention, Bev realized that it was somehow fitting. It was like a representation of Hal's brain.

"Come in, come in," he continued to usher her to the kitchen area. It was much neater than the living room. Pots on the stove bubbled with red thick sauces and steaming pasta. There were candles lit on the table and wine ready to be poured.

"Everything is about ready. Wine?" She hesitated, she really wanted this to be an eating meeting, not a wine and dine date. He read her mind. "Come on, no funny business. You can't have Italian without a great Merlot." He poured and handed her a glass.

"Thank you, where did you learn to cook?"

He offered her a chair and continued the meal prep.

"My Mom, she loved to cook and I loved to watch her. She showed me most of what I know. Italian is my specialty." He bowed with flare, his long arms waving a wooden spoon for effect.

Bev laughed. She imagined a crane like hippy Mom, teaching her little crane to cook. She really did like Hal, but Sam had gotten under her skin. She began to doubt her judgment in anything.

"How's the historical piece going?" Hal strode around the kitchen draining pasta, tossing salad, and checking the bread in the oven.

"Fine, I got a lot done the other night, stayed up late, things were just flowing."

He refilled her glass. "I love when that happens. It's like energy flowing through your finger tips that magically turns into words on the page. I love that..." He stopped and contemplated the idea, downed his glass of wine and went back to the meal.

"Hmm, yes. So tell me what your thoughts are on the arson recap." She took a small piece of bread out of the basket he set on the table.

"Yeah, yeah...I want to do a detailed time line with any new evidence added in, who knows maybe it will unlock someone's memory on a lost fact. Plus it was a huge event this year and I want to milk it for all it's worth." Hal set a plate of ravioli in front of her and took his to his place and sat down.

"We can lay it out after dinner, bon appetite." He winked and clinked her glass with his.

"Wow, it looks incredible." She dug in.

"You look incredible." He wasn't eating, just staring at her.

"Hal, you promised," she scolded.

"Sorry, momentary lapse... so how is super cop?" He chomped on some bread.

"Also not fair, I'm not going there with you."

"Ok, Ok! Just business."

THEY MOVED their meeting to the living room after dinner. They had finished the first bottle of wine and were well into their second. Hal had an amazing way of drawing her into a story, she could tell that he was a skilled journalist.

"Have you ever thought of writing a novel?" She was full and relaxed and finely in no hurry to go anywhere, just exchange ideas with a fellow writer.

"I have one in the works."

They sat across from each other in what appeared to be recently excavated seating. The area around the fireplace was also cleared and a roaring blaze cast shadows off the books onto the tin ceiling above.

"Really! What's the story line?" She sat up ready to be entertained.

"A work in progress, sort of pieces of a story really. Have you ever written one?" He solemnly watched a log roll up against the grate.

"That could be dangerous in here," she teased, regretting saying it the moment it left her lips. He looked at her for a moment, his gaze was unusually dark as he stood to tend the fire.

"No, I don't have a whole story either." She tried to recover the moment with inane blather, "Maybe you have to live a whole story to write one."

His back was to her but she noticed him cock his head thinking.

"Maybe."

When he turned she didn't like the look on his face, it was different, predatory. Surely he wasn't that touchy about his housekeeping. Maybe the wine was getting to him. The silence between them was becoming awkward.

"May I use your restroom?" She broke his gaze looking around for the right trail to the powder room.

"Sure, down the hall to the left."

She maneuvered herself out of his way, glad for the escape. "Wow, moody," she thought as she tended to her business.

Unfortunately, like most men, Hal had forgotten to restock the toilet paper for his female guest. She opened nearby cabinets searching. Lots of bottles of old shampoo, a half empty case of cigarettes, plungers, cleaners. Nothing within reach. She dripped dry well enough but was determined to help the next unsuspecting guest. Finally under the sink she found a half roll and gladly put it on the holder.

"Men," she thought as she primped and washed her hands. This time there was no towel handy so she opened the cabinet behind her. Good, towels. Odd, she wondered why Hal had cleaners in with the towels. She grabbed the opaque gallon jug with clear liquid to put it under the sink with other like items. The label caught her eye. She had seen this same jug before somewhere recently.

"You all right in there? Did you fall in?" Hal snickered out in the hall.

"Be right out."

Bev turned the bottle around. Acetone.

Acetone?

She was suddenly acutely sober. She had seen this very bottle in the store room at the newspaper. Used for transfer of ink, highly flammable, Molotov cocktails, someone who had something to gain from setting the fires. Her mind was whirling. Panic started to build.

"Hal?" She thought, unbelieving.

He knocked and she jumped. Hal. She opened the door suddenly causing him to jump back. He was drunk, she had to leave.

"Hal, I'm not feeling very well."

She pushed past him, but although her mind was sharp her body was still feeling the effects of the wine. He caught her as she stumbled over a stack of books against the wall. She was wrapped in his arms before she could get out of the hallway.

"Bev." He said softly. Her heart was beating wildly. Did he know that she knew? "I can't give you up. We are so good together." He stroked her hair, she tried not to wince but she felt certain the fear was showing on her face. "I want to write my story with you." He kissed her softly and slowly. Bev could hear herself screaming in her own head. The adrenaline was pumping, she was breathing in shallow breaths. "Oh Bev," he was misinterpreting her fear for passion. She glanced into the bathroom. She could see the Acetone on the counter.

"A barn burner, it's my paper, I'll milk it for all it's

worth." Hals own words were flooding back to her. God she wanted Sam. She could play it cool, she could even sleep with Hal if she had to get away when he fell asleep. She would be cool.

"Hal," she cleared her throat, she even sounded scared, hell, she was scared. He followed her glance in the reflection of the mirror on the door of the bathroom. She could almost see the cogs in his brain following the trail. The light shifted in his eyes and he looked down at her and tightened his grip around her.

"Well, aren't you the little investigative journalist?" His smile was wild and flashing. She feigned ignorance.

"What are you talking about? I thought we were talking about us." She pressed up against him, she was pretty sure the act was unconvincing, but surprisingly he softened his grip and kissed her again. His kiss, however, was malicious and she knew instantly this wasn't going to end well.

He laughed out loud at the look on her face. He took her by the wrists and literally drug her to the living room, knocking over stacks of books and papers in their wake.

"Hal! Stop it! Let me go!" She struggled against him, she would have never guessed he was this strong.

"Oh no, darlin', don't think so." He held her at arm's length, gripping both her wrists with the long fingers of one of his long hands, searching his desk with his free hand.

"Hal! You can't seriously want to hurt me, after everything we've shared."

He snorted, "You self-righteous bitch." He didn't even turn to speak to her while he continued to search. "You never cared for me, it's been that son of bitch cop this whole time. What a joke. He and the rest of this town are pathetic. Do you know how easy it has been to fool them all?"

His hair was as wild as the look on his face, the fireplace

lit him with a red glow from behind. How could she have not seen this before? The man was demented! Without ceremony he suddenly held up the roll of duct tape that had been the object of the search and slammed it against her face. She felt herself go limp, a stack of papers breaking her fall. Then blackness.

24

Finally the last guests found their wraps and made their way to the front of the hotel. The newly engaged hosts bid each good night and carefully closed the beautiful oak doors behind them.

Silence filled the grand hall. Jacob took Netty's hand and kissed it.

"Thank you, my darling." Jacob's charm was undeniable. "I couldn't have done it without you."

She smiled knowingly.

"Of course you couldn't," she thought to herself, letting him flatter her. It was a silly game, she knew, allowing herself to feel something for him. She told herself it helped keep up the deception. Jacob moved closer, embracing her.

"We are going to be incredibly happy." His eyes were intent, serious. "You are incredibly beautiful." She let him kiss her, losing herself just for a moment in his searching mouth.

"Jacob," she whispered, he kissed her again. This time she stiffened under his demanding hold and drew back.

"Jacob, please!" She pulled away.

"Oh, Netty, I'm just so happy. I want to show you how much you mean to me." He smiled warmly and closed in on her again.

"Jacob," she placed a hand on his chest, she could feel the blood pulsing through his heart. He wasn't going to be put off easily. He pushed her against the velvet papered wall and kissed her face, her neck and mouth. She closed her eyes, their breathing matching their increasing desire.

"Not yet," came a small voice from her conscience. Jacob expertly began making his way around her weskit and skirt laces.

"Not yet," the voice cried louder, her hair was falling free from its combs. Suddenly she saw his face, blond curls blowing in a spring breeze, "Jace!" She said it out loud and drew a sharp breath. "No!" She reared back and struck her new husband-to-be across the face.

For a moment Jacob was stunned, then he grabbed both her forearms in a quick angry response, holding her there against the wall. A red welt instantly began to flush his cheek. He paused as he stared at her, eyes blazing with anger, desire and lust. His breathing slowed and he regained his composure. A broadening grin spread across his face matching the sting from her slap.

"Oh, I think yes," he said slowly, narrowing his gaze.

The wolf shed his sheep's clothes so quickly Netty didn't recognize him. He forced her back against the wall kissing her harder till she thought she couldn't breathe. He used his hip and one hand to pin her there, handily finishing undressing her to the waist with the other. She found herself going numb, shocked that it was happening this way. She began to protest again but too late. He slapped her face and threw her onto the beautiful ruby carpet.

"I have waited long enough, my dear. Shall we make our

engagement official?" He leered at her and was upon her before she could move away.

She couldn't respond, she couldn't defend herself, it was as if all of her energy was drained away. She was losing control of all she had worked toward. Jace's cherubic face danced in her mind, beckoning her to come with him. How she wished she could. She lay motionless as he jutted and pulled at her. What had made her think she could repay such sorrow with deception and cruelty? How had she thought this was going to end?

End it did, just as suddenly as Jacob had moved upon her, the act was finished. He moved away and stood up. She continued to lay still not wanting to agitate him in any way, like a wounded animal playing dead. She could feel him watching her as he buttoned his trousers and vest.

"Jace." His voice sounded so large and so out of context saying the name for a moment she thought she had heard it in her mind. "Jace? Poor Jace." His tone was mocking. She finally turned to look at Jacob's face to be sure the words were actually coming from his mouth. "Only Jace I know is, or should I say *was*, was Jace Caverson." He paused for effect checking his hair and tending a small scratch Netty had managed to inflict during the struggle. "My father shot him, he was a thief." He turned and leveled his gaze to hers. "Then you shot my father."

For the second time that evening she felt herself going numb. She blinked, covering herself, trying not to let everything be exposed about her at once.

He came at her again, making her flinch. "Did you think I wouldn't find out? Netty Bingham Caverson? My darling bride to be?" He laughed. "Don't worry, I'm not angry at you for killing him, he was a bastard. And if you hadn't, we wouldn't have all this," he gestured to the grand room around them and all its appointments, but meaning the sordid interchange between them. "The beauty of it is, that we are truly two of a kind. Out to get our own way, not caring who we use or step on to get there. I look forward to many years of our union."

He extended his hand to lift her from the floor. She didn't move. He finally shrugged and, laughing, turned to go out.

"Now, my dear, I have a previously scheduled appointment. Plan our wedding for next week, what do you think?" He winked and left her alone in the foyer of the grand hotel.

25

One, two, three florescent lamps. Four, five, six. They passed overhead as she was being wheeled quickly through the grey halls. She could not see who was pushing and there was no sound. Where was she? A hospital...she could smell the cleaners, the alcohol, the passing of life to death. Everything was so bright under the bare lights, she wanted to ask what was going on but couldn't find her voice. The gurney suddenly stopped. She waited a moment then sat up slowly. There was no orderly, no one in the nurse's station, the only sound her own breathing.

It was as if she was moving in slow motion as she let herself off the rolling bed.

Knowingly, Bev turned down a corridor that was darker than the rest of the wards on the floor. Only one room cast light into the hallway. Slowly she moved toward it, fearful of what she would find but compelled to go. Her heart beat in her chest mixing with the sound of her increased breathing inside her head. As she reached the doorway only the sound of her heart fluttering could be heard as she held her breath.

Relief overcame her and her breathing continued as soon as she entered the room, suddenly realizing why she was there.

Her father lay in the narrow railed bed, head slightly elevated, his skin the same color as the tightly fitted sheets that held him there.

"He's alive," she thought, relieved.

She quickly moved to his side taking his hand. It was cool, still large and reassuring, his wrists and forearms, however, looked small and frail. Thankfully, he was sleeping peacefully, his chest rising and falling in an easy rhythm. His face looked old and drawn, blue veins showing through white lashed eyelids. Wires and tubes led from him to various machines that were pumping and pulsing. Their curious silence didn't relieve her anxiety.

"Bev," his distinct baritone whispered her name inside her head. She could feel the tears begin to well behind her eyes. She wanted to answer but could not make a sound. She drew closer holding his hand to her heart, gazing into his light blue eyes.

"Bev, I love you." He smiled broadly, squeezing her hand slightly. Oh how she loved him, why couldn't she say it to him?

"I've got to go," he continued, wincing slightly and closing his eyes. She felt her heart drop, screaming in her head "NO! Not yet! There's so much to say!"

"Bev, I'm sorry," he sighed heavily, "so sorry."

"There's no need." She clung to his arm, pleading with her eyes, shaking her head.

"So sorry..." his words trailed off this time, his hand and arm relaxed.

"This can't be happening again." She rubbed his arm, patted his hand, and stroked his face, finally turning to check the now inactive silent machines.

"No...no!" She shook her head madly, where was everyone, nurses, doctors?

She couldn't find the strength to let go of his hand to go and look for help, terrified to leave him. Instead she lay her head on his broad chest, closing her eyes.

"Oh Dad, no, I'm sorry. I love you." She wept bitterly, eyes shut tight.

Darkness and tears were her only solace now. The grief came in waves, rushes of anguish rolling out of her heart with every tear until it slowed and then stopped, exhausted. She stayed there, not moving, for what seemed like a very long time, finally falling asleep like she used to as a child, resting her head on him.

"Bev, I love you," she heard again, comforted by his last words. "I'm sorry," also echoed in her head, piercing her heart anew.

"No need..." she whispered, this time her words were audible.

"I'm sorry I got you into this," the tone in his voice confused her, she struggled to open her eyes to look at him. Was he speaking or was she just imagining it?

There was a fog in the room dimming the harsh hospital light. Her throat was so dry. The crying had dehydrated her, parching her mouth and lips.

"I love you, Bev."

Suddenly she recognized the voice, it wasn't her Father speaking. Sam. She blinked frantically trying to see him. How did he know where to find her? She couldn't move, couldn't see. A wave of panic came over her and she began to struggle to stand up. She drew in a sharp breath wanting to call out but her lungs were filled with stinging smoke. Coughing and gagging, she came into full consciousness.

Her eyes were covered with something, tape. The

memory of the roll of tape flashed in her mind. Her legs were also bound in front of her at the ankle and the knee, presumably also with tape. Her hands – she struggled to pull them from behind her.

Sam groaned. My God, she was tied to Sam! Even in her dreamy stupor the puzzle wasn't that hard to put together. Hal had somehow gotten she and Sam here and had set a fire intending to kill them both. Hoping to make headlines once again and inflicting his personal vendetta all at once.

"Sam," she croaked out, wiggling her hands, wrapping her fingers in his. She could feel sweat and something stickier, blood, on his hands and hers.

"Sam!" She screamed with all the air left in her lungs setting off another coughing fit. His hands reacted to hers but his shoulders slumped away, he was unconscious. A wave of adrenaline shot through her, her brain shifted into high gear, survival instinct took over. The thought of Sam and the pain in her shoulders and wrists drove her frenzy.

She twisted her slippery wrists back and forth, the tape was giving way. The heat in the room was rising quickly, she could hear the crackle of flame and wood. She was getting dizzy from tainted oxygen and a head injury that throbbed mercilessly. Still she pulled and twisted trying to breathe through her nose. The big cop at her back helped counter weight her efforts.

"Pull dammit," she commanded herself. Tears of fear streamed down her cheeks. Suddenly her one arm snapped free. She and Sam fell onto their shoulders, she clawed at the tape on her face with her free hand still twisting the hand under her. In one swift movement her eyes and hands were free. She surveyed the room as she ripped the tape that bound her legs.

She had no idea where they were. A large old building,

lots of boxes, tires, barrels. Oh God... her heart sunk, it was a car garage or a storage facility for automotive junk. So many flammables. Flames were lapping everywhere, the smoke was turning from grey to black, burning her eyes and lungs.

Sam lay in a fetal position, his broad shoulders to her, hands trussed with cuffs behind his back. "Oh God, Sam!" She went to him, carefully examining his neck and head. He had a large gash over one eye and on the back of his head. The blood had soaked the collar of his uniform and continued down his back. His wrists were cut from struggling against the cuffs. The head wounds were not bleeding anymore and there were no other signs of injury. Like her, he was struggling to breath. She searched his pockets for his keys, they had to be his cuffs. Certainly Hal wouldn't have been so sadistic as to own his own pair. No keys. She stroked his face, he was smudged with grease, ash and blood.

"How did Hal get him here?" She stood, "We have to get out."

The fire was moving fast from one end of the building, barring the only visible door. It was beginning to climb the far wall to the roof. She moved frantically around the stacks of boxes, no exits on the other side except two garage doors with small windows in the top. She raced to try and open them. Locked by Hal or stuck from years of no use, she couldn't budge them. There was no way to get an unconscious or even a conscious Sam through those windows. A flash of a reflection caught her eye. The fire was reflecting off a car. She covered her mouth and nose with her elbow and stumbled to it.

Sam's police car! She fell into the driver's seat. "Keys, keys, keys – please." The thickening smoke and fading daylight were closing in, she was running out of time.

Wouldn't the fire department be called? She strained to

hear the sound of rescue but heard none. They were obviously outside of town, Hal would have made sure help would never get there in time.

A huge explosion shook the building behind her, sending her to the floorboard under the dash, sounds of ominously hissing liquids and creaking timber followed.

"Oh God, please!" She was openly sobbing and choking. Her hands flew over the dashboard, under the seat and finally in the ignition her hand hit the key.

She plopped down in the seat, slammed her foot on the clutch and turned the engine over. She left it running and ran back to Sam. He was still laying where she had left him. She pulled him from his shoulder, falling backward on the floor.

Shit! He was too heavy, she tried from his feet with no luck.

Sweat was pouring down her face into her already stinging eyes. Desperately she shook his shoulders, screaming his name. No response. There was too much debris, she couldn't get the car to him, she would have to move him.

Flinging open boxes she looked for something to slide him on. Nothing. Then against the wall she saw it. A mechanic's chassis. Precious seconds were spent getting to it and getting it to him. She was coughing with every breath now. She sat him up and with some difficulty lay him back on his side on the rolling platform. He was wheezing with every breath, his chest heaving like a fish out of water. Half dragging half rolling, she moved him painstakingly toward the car, staying low, hoping for more oxygen near the floor. Once she had to reposition him when he fell off. He never flinched, never called out.

"Please don't die," she pleaded with him as she turned

the car off and used the keys to unlock the cuffs. Luckily the car was low, the chassis slid right up to the floorboard. One limb at a time she moved him, rolling him into the reclined seat and forcing the door shut behind him. She didn't notice the surface of the car was hot to the touch until she let herself in the driver's side. A wall of flames was feet from the car, the area where they had been bound was completely engulfed. She restarted the car and looked in the rear view mirror. The only way out was through the old garage door behind her. Surely this power house could punch through the aging wall. She had no other choice.

She revved the engine as if she was a teenage street racer, feeling the power of the engine, reassuring herself. She pushed Sam back as far as she could in the seat, he was in the belt but would surely fly forward with the impact.

She was out of time, the roof was giving way.

"One ...Two... Three!" She slammed the car into reverse, letting the clutch fly and floored the gas. The mustang lunged backwards, there was twenty feet to build momentum, it happened in seconds. The back end smashed into the garage door, folding it in and over them, sparks and flames shot out chasing them from the building and, as if on cue, the wall of the storage building collapsed inward. A huge black cloud lifted into the evening sky.

Bev had the gas to the floor, putting as much distance between them and the fire as she could. It occurred to her too late that there may be other obstacles in her path. The second she thought to look behind her she saw the tree and simultaneously smashed the car into it full force. The last thing she saw was the airbag rushing up to certainly smother her in a starry flash.

26

Clint Murray had made it half way back to the ranch when he suddenly pulled his horse around and headed back to town. The images of Jacob petting and holding Netty at the party rolled over and over in his head. How had his weasel brother turned her head? He was nothing but a lazy, cheating self-serving fool. There seemed no end to the favor he had found in this town portraying himself as a reputable businessman and life partner for Netty. Blocking Clint's attempted success at both. He knew Netty was no innocent in this either, he was not that naive, he just couldn't understand why. The more he thought about it the more he hated them both.

He left his horse at the edge of town. The streets were dark, the hour was very late or very early, he had lost track. He kept to the shadows of the buildings until he was directly across from the Belle Hotel. The lights were still on in the main foyer. Surely the guests had left for the evening, his round trip had taken almost two hours. Suddenly the upstairs room lights went on. Netty was there, was she alone? Of course, the woman he knew was upstanding and gentile, just misguided. Maybe she could still be convinced she was making a mistake. After all, what did he have to lose?

He waited, watching the window. He saw her shadow move in the room. She had hurt him so deeply, led him to believe she cared, but why? She could have told him from the beginning that she didn't want him but she kept yanking him around misleading him. Had Jacob convinced her that somehow he wasn't worthy? That had to be it.

He would go to her, find out what lies his brother had told about him and renew her faith in him. He stepped out to cross the street when he noticed the lights go out. He stepped back, maybe he would have to wait until morning, get a room for the night. No he must speak to her now. He decided to go around the back of the hotel, perhaps she had left her window open and he could get her attention.

Netty lay still on the floor for a long time. How could she let it come to this? This twist of plot was never anticipated, she had never considered that Jacob would discover her identity. What a fool she'd been to underestimate the greedy distrusting nature of a man. She had thought of him as an ignorant, if not driven, fool. She had not thought beyond their betrothal to an actual wedding or marriage other than to hold Jacob responsible for Jace's death and force him to "pay" daily for the rest of his life. Did she have any leverage left? It didn't seem likely. It was even too late to bring Clint back into the scene to help her. The play was over, she would be Jacob's puppet instead. She felt desperate and alone.

She pulled herself up, every part of her body felt heavy.

She turned out the hall light and made her way upstairs. Every step was an effort. It seemed a lifetime ago that she had gloried at the top of the beautiful staircase even though it had been just hours before.

Her apartment was dark. She lit the lamp at the dressing table and tentatively looked in the mirror, dreading the revelation she would see there. She was a tattered mess, her hair fallen, her face, neck and breasts bruised, the red dress torn and stained. The tears finally started to fall, first from shock and pain and then from anger. How could he? How could he treat her this way? As she undressed in front of the mirror, bruises began to pool all over her body under her fair skin. Her anger fumed, then sparked and finally burned. No man could do this to her without penalty.

She washed, she scrubbed, everywhere he had touched her. This incident would change nothing. She still had her rage if not her dignity and the only way to regain all that Jacob Murray had taken from her was to use that rage.

She would play the dutiful wife, she would bide her time, he had no idea of her resolve, her real motives. He thought he could play her, take her life, her body, and break her. He had no idea. She dressed her wounds, and put on her night clothes, she was suddenly exhausted from the drama of the day. She locked the apartment door and was turning to go to bed when she heard voices downstairs.

She extinguished the lamp and opened the door quietly listening intently. She didn't have the strength to fight off thieves or dissuade unruly party goers coming back for another round. The tone of the visitors, however, was not threatening, they were obviously friendly, a woman and a man. Lovers unaware that the hotel was not yet open for business. The front hall was still lit, she must not have locked the front door. She reached for her robe, knowing this wouldn't be the first time her evening would be interrupted if she intended to be a hotel owner.

She was about to speak out to the couple when she recognized the man's voice. Jacob. He was speaking low and inviting, a tone she was not unfamiliar with and she knew immediately the woman was Janine, the whore from the bar. He had brought her here. They were slipping into one of the downstairs rooms.

He brought her here. The thought was nauseating. After everything that had happened this evening? A heat rose from her pounding heart, the black ink that had been quelled there temporarily by hurt and disbelief began to overflow. She wanted him gone, gone forever. He was vile, she had always known it, she had just momentarily forgotten. Her thoughts flew.

It would be easy to kill him, there was a pistol at the front desk, and no one would charge the betrayed fiance. The perfect solution. Her real identity would never be revealed. Jace's death would be repaid. It would close the curtain on this play. She could run the Belle as she wanted immediately instead of being at the mercy of the hand of this pig for a lifetime. She silently descended the stairs, quickly found the gun and went to the door of their room.

CLINT LIT a small piece of kindling wood from the lantern on the street and walked around the row of buildings next to the Belle. It wasn't hard to pick out the new construction from the back and discern which second story window was probably Netty's.

Clint hesitated. Was he sure he had a chance?

The woman in the letters had encouraged his attentions,

flattered him, and enticed him. Was he that big of a fool? She had to have been deceived by Jacob, there was no other explanation. He still had a chance.

"Netty," he whispered loudly, "Netty!" he tried a little louder. The window curtains moved in the night breeze, he listened intently for any sound from the room that she may be coming.

None.

"Netty!" He half spoke waving his small torch and listened again. He heard a woman's voice this time. "It's me Clint." He heard a voice again, this time joined by another and realized it wasn't coming from upstairs but from one of the downstairs rooms nearer him.

He laid his light down on the gravel and edged closer. The room was barely lit, he could not see its occupants from his angle. It was a man and a woman. Jacob and Netty? The two were lost in love making, making coy suggestions and laughing softly.

"No," thought Clint, "not Netty." His mind reeled again with rejection and anger. So this was her choice? This was the woman she really was.

He was disgusted at them both. He could hear them getting more and more intimate, images of them splashed across his mind. He had been completely taken, felt like a fool, and he had lost. They had deceived and manipulated him and they had won. Whatever affection he felt for Netty vanished.

In a sudden act of jealousy he grabbed the fire stick, he would burn this place to the ground. This monument to greed, betrayal, and lust would be nothing but ash when he was finished. He fed the flame of the torch with a rag from the ash bin and raised back to throw it into the window.

SHE LISTENED to the couple laugh and taunt one another. Sounds of coupling, the bed frame creaking, moans of pleasure. Netty thought she may be sick not from jealousy but from pure disgust. She waited, waited for them both to be completely indisposed. She would shoot them both. She heard Janine coo and sigh at his touch, she heard him groan and breathe heavily.

She cocked the gun and slowly turned the door knob. The new hardware on the door was silent, the only light was one small lamp dimly lit on the far nightstand. She could see their silhouette, naked and entwined.

She did not know it was possible to hate someone as much as she hated Jacob Murray at that moment. She leveled the pistol, one shot might kill them both through their torsos but she wanted to be sure he was the main target. She aimed at the back of his head, he was lost in the throes of passion but to her he was no more than an unwanted stray dog. A snap of the cartridge, a flash of powder and the bullet hit its target, as well as the state of the art gas line in the wall behind him. The explosion was immense, knocking Netty unconscious as it threw her out into the foyer and engulfing the Belle in flames.

27

Fragments. Bits and pieces of light and sound. Every sense acutely aware but unable to send identifiable signals to the brain. Loud grinding, sharp mind altering pain, noxious smells and tastes, flashing images. Jesus Martinez in full fire gear, reassuring her with words but with unconvincing expressions and movements. A twisted wreck of black and white wrapped up and around the trunk of an old oak tree. People and shadows flitting in front of a huge orange and black sky. Please let it be a dream. Finally deep, dark, thoughtless sleep.

Bev moved in and out of consciousness. Nothing was concrete, she would open her eyes but could not comprehend what she saw, familiar words and voices occasionally broke through but only for a moment. Even the bed she rested on seemed to float up and away at times. Slowly she began to realize the difference between pain and no pain, cold and warmth, light and dark. Slowly the thickness in her head began to give way to clear lines of thinking.

Three days after the wreck she opened her eyes in El

Paso General Hospital and the memories began to flood back, she and Sam in the car, racing away from the fire.

"How did they get there? Hal. Where was Sam?" It hurt to think or keep her eyes open.

"Sam," she whispered. Monitors around her set off a series of beeps and increased vibrations. A nurse entered promptly.

"Hello Mrs. Connors. I'm Diane one of your night nurses," she spoke in hushed tones and checked Bev's vitals on the machines. "How are you feeling?" The question seemed ridiculous but necessary.

"Foggy." Bev was surprised she could be so descriptive. "Sam Gant?" She managed.

"You rest, the doctor and the sheriff will be in to see you in the morning." Nurse Diane manipulated the fluids in Bev's IV and she drifted back into oblivion.

SHE WOKE to two men standing at the foot of her bed. Both looked concerned, both smiling benevolently. One was her doctor, she guessed from his garb. The other was Officer Mac.

The Doctor took charge coming to her side. "Mrs. Connors? So good to see you alert." He flashed a pin light in each of her eyes and looked at her hands on top and bottom. "Do you remember how you got here?" Mac stood dutifully by, hat in hand, waiting his turn.

"Not how, but I remember the fire, the car wreck...where's Sam?" She looked at Mac for the answer, praying he wasn't there officially. The Doctor graciously referred the question to him.

"Sam's here. Down the hall. He's hurt but not as bad as

you, he has been asking to come see you." Mac smiled weakly. Her heart heaved a sigh of relief.

The Doctor took his cue. "You have multiple contusions to the head, neck and spinal bruising, 2nd degree burns on your hands and neck and a broken hip."

"My God," she thought.

"No wonder I feel like hell," she commented. Both men smiled, hoping her show of spunk was an indicator that she wasn't going to wither under her recovery. "What about Hal? This was all Hal." Mac was nodding as she said it.

"We know. Sam had been on his tail for several days when he disappeared." He patted her hand.

"Did you get him?" She had so many questions but was already getting winded.

Mac's face changed to angry disappointment. "No, he disappeared and then the fire and your injuries. I was hoping you might remember something." His eyebrows raised hopefully.

"I remember the dinner we had, I found acetone in his bathroom in a jug like the ones in the press room, he boasted that he had set the fires for headlines. I don't remember anything about how he got me to the warehouse, sorry." He kept patting her hand.

"That's good enough for now. You rest, we'll talk more later. I'll tell Sam you're back with us." He left the room.

The Doctor stepped back to her side, "I am giving you Hydrocodone for the pain. You will have surgery on your hip tomorrow, we had to wait until you were conscious again and the swelling on your neck and spine went down." He typed into a bedside computer as he spoke, "I'll allow clear fluids today and I want you to sleep as much as possible."

She nodded, wanting to close her eyes as he said it. "Shouldn't be a problem," she mumbled. "Where was Hal?"

She thought to herself, seeing his wild hair and face with fire lit sky behind him as she fell back to sleep.

SURGERY PREP, procedure and post op came and went without much conscious effort on Bev's part. Frankly she was glad for the mind numbing painkillers and the chance for deep slumber. She resisted none of the suggestions from her nurses and doctors as to medication doses or frequency. The day after surgery, however, when rehab began and Beverly started to wonder if any of it was worth it. She began to hate the tiny athletic Hispanic woman, Josey, who was in charge of her torture.

"Ms. Connors, today we are going to stand and learn to pivot to the bedside commode," Josey said matter-of-factly.

"Great." Bev was less than enthusiastic. Really, who could get excited about a bedside toilet!

"I will be here to support you, but I want you to try to bear most of the weight on your good leg." She was putting a belt around Bev's middle, she felt a bit like a downed horse being cinched.

"Sure." It hadn't been that long ago that she had done therapy on the "good" leg for her knee and ankle, she was running out of "good" legs.

With a bit of shuffling and puffing, Bev managed to stand, pivot and sit. She was appalled at her own weakness and sat dizzy on the commode for some time before trying a return run.

"Wow, I am so weak," she confessed to Josey.

"Everyone starts out that way, you'll be amazed at how fast you recover. You're tough and strong. It will all be good." Josey volunteered a smile. Bev was pretty sure that she had to say these things so people didn't fall into despondency over having to use a bedside toilet.

Bev quickly found out how and how not to shift her hip, or where to put pressure on her sensitive hands. Somehow she got back in a prone position in the bed, sweating and winded. Her lungs ached from the effort, no doubt a by-product of smoke inhalation.

"I will be back later." Josey expertly shifted IV tubing and bedding around her patient. "If you need to use the toilet in between, call the nurse's station."

At this moment, Bev was sure she wouldn't have to go again until tomorrow.

"Thank you, I will." Josey left her after updating the computer chart. Bev closed her eyes.

"Man, this is going to take a while," she thought. In a minute it didn't seem to matter as her latest dose of painkiller kicked in. She was drifting off to sleep. She could smell fresh grass, saw the stars twinkling in the night sky, she felt warmth and Sam's face appeared, looking like he did that night, he was smiling knowingly and his eyes twinkled mischievously.

"Bev?" She heard him whisper. It was so real she could smell him, feel his hand on her face.

"Bev?" She opened her eyes, his face was there, he was there.

"Sam." She was so glad to see him. He smiled. Relieved. She tried to focus. "Sorry, I'm kind of out of it." He leaned over and kissed her forehead, pausing there for a moment. Her eyes began to pool. He was Ok.

"I thought..." he choked up and looked away for a moment. He cleared his throat, "Thanks."

She noticed the bandages on his head and the shadows

of two black eyes. She patted his hand on the bed with her mitt covered hand.

"I know, it was touch and go for us both for a while. Are you Ok?" She recovered for them both, he smiled warmly and sat on the edge of the bed.

"You do care," he teased gently. "Yes. I'm good. Concussion, two broken ribs and a dislocated shoulder." Bev cringed for a moment, thinking of his unconscious fall to the shoulder.

"I'm on the mend, I was released yesterday. Just out patient rehab for the shoulder, on sick leave from work until the ribs heal a bit." He was accessing her injuries as he was talking. Turning her bandaged hand in his. "How's the hip?" He asked.

God, he smelled good. "I must look and smell like night of the dead." She thought, suddenly conscious of personal hygiene.

"Sore, I got up today for the first time." She felt like an old woman talking about her ailments. "I'm tough, it will all be good," quoting Josey.

"Tell me what happened." She focused back on his beautiful face.

"Now? Are you sure you're up to it?" He brushed the hair off her forehead.

"You have my full attention until the pain meds knock me out." She grinned, meeting his gaze directly. She felt like anything was possible if he was there. "Start by telling me where you went and why you didn't return my calls." His eyebrows rose, and he sat back in the chair and chuckled.

"You're going to be fine, Beverly Connors." He took a deep relieved breath and began to fill in the blanks with his story.

28

There was a "snap" and then the concussion of the explosion threw Clint back against the far wall of the building on the opposite side of the alley. His ears were ringing, the breath knocked out of his lungs. The flames shot out of the downstairs window toward him causing him to scramble backwards along the ground, finally he gained his footing and was able to turn and run. As he turned the corner onto the main street, sleepy store owners and stunned late night patrons of Charlie's were stumbling into the street, trying to comprehend the scene in front of them. As if in a silent slow motion movie, people began to react.

The newly varnished and painted walls of the Belle hotel fueled the fireball, burning first blue, then crimson, then white. By the time the fire line had been organized and the first bucket of water had been tossed futilely into the foyer, fire was rising up the beautiful stairway and lighting the entire street through the front windows. Blistering, blinding heat and flames.

Clint watched, dumb struck. He tried to comprehend

what had happened, how had the fire started? His torch? It had to be the gas, his torch had set it off.

Clint came out of his shock as someone asked, "Where are Miss Bingham and Mr. Murray?"

"My God," thought Clint. He began to run to the front of the hotel.

"They're still inside!" Screamed a woman. Someone tried to pull him back but he ripped free, covering his face with his sleeve against the searing heat. The front doors had been blown open by the blast. He could barely stand to look through the heat and smoke. He could feel his exposed skin burning. The downstairs bedroom was engulfed, she and Jacob had no chance. In horror he began to turn back when he saw the edge of a woman's gown and an exposed foot.

"Netty." His heart swelled, stripping off his coat, he dunked it in a bucket, covered his head and plowed head-long into the heat and flames. She had been thrown against the front wall of the foyer, the fire had not yet reached her. She looked like a child's doll that had been carelessly discarded on the floor. He rushed to her, not yet feeling the sting in his eyes or lungs, scooped her up and flung himself through the closest window, covering her with his own body and the coat. He collapsed to his knees when he reached the middle of the street, people came running to their aid.

He looked at her pale face, her golden hair fanned out around her shoulders, and he began to cry. How could he have thought to harm her? She had not been in the back room with Jacob. Who was Jacob with?

He turned to look at the fire. The whole two story building was blazing, all was lost. All the grandeur, the carved woodwork, the art, the deep red carpets, all gone. The fire line had turned its attention to neighboring buildings trying to prevent the fire from spreading. Jacob was surely dead as was his consort.

Netty began to choke and gasp as she regained consciousness. He went to her side.

"Miss Bingham, try not to move. We'll get you to Doc Parson's office." She did not respond, laying back on the stretcher, coughing violently. Clint watched her disappear into the fire lit night.

He sat back down in the center of the street, suddenly exhausted, and wept like he was a ten-year old boy. He felt so betrayed, so confused, so lost. The accumulation of all his recent defeats came bubbling up out of his soul. The loss of his father, the near loss of the ranch, the loss of Netty, the loss of his only brother, and the loss of his pride. He felt whipped and scorched by the fire and by life. He watched the town's people scurry like so many ants having lost the fight but refusing to give in.

Could he go on? He thought about Netty again, she was still alive but he had nearly killed her. It was all his fault, she would never have him now. He must have caused the blaze, a gas leak must have reached his torch. How could this happen, why him, the "good" son, the faithful suitor, an upright citizen.

He heard his father's voice in his head, "Stand up son." He slowly did as he was told, wiping his face and nose with his sleeve.

He knew what he must do. He would confess, he would make it right. That was all that he had left, to do the right thing, to be right with her. He would go to her, tell her what he had done and let her determine his fate.

The raging flames continued through the night ripping through five of the main street buildings. It depleted men's energy, their water and their dreams in its wake. A pale sun rose on what was left of a smoldering defeated western town filled with ash covered, disillusioned town folk.

Everyone was asking the same questions. "What had happened, how had the fire started?" and resounding their condolences, "Poor Mr. Murray", "Pray for Miss Bingham".

Desperation began to fill hearts, fuel fears, and drive fury. The answers needed to be found.

29

Sam recounted his surveillance of Hal Preston. His suspicions had been aroused when Hal had come into the station the day after the last fire. Hal had been almost giddy with the prospect of writing the story. Sam had intended to tell Bev he was going undercover the night that he had seen she and Hal lip locked in her kitchen. Bev tried to defend her actions, but he re-assured her it didn't take long for him to figure out that she and Hal were not an item and that Hal was dangerous. He had seen that Bev tried to contact him, but he didn't want Hal to connect the two of them, little did he know that he already had.

There were many mundane hours of sitting outside the newspaper office and Hal's remote home. Sam had misjudged Hal's intelligence, a big mistake. He had just checked in with dispatch about 2am when he was injected in the neck through the open window of his car where he had been sitting down the road from Hal's house. The drug had worked quickly, Sam didn't have a chance to draw a gun or call out on the radio. By the time Mac figured out where

Sam was, Bev was in Hal's house and they didn't want to spook him.

Sam had come to in a room filled top to bottom with books and papers, he assumed it

was in Hal's house. He had been trussed and cuffed and try as he might he couldn't get loose. The worst part was he could hear Bev and Hal's muffled voices at dinner that night, he had tried to make noise but the books were very effective sound proofing. The last time Sam saw Hal, he had a baseball bat. Mac never did figure out how Hal had gotten the two of them and the police car past them to the warehouse.

Bev was breathing heavily. She had made it through Sam's narrative to the part where he was tied up in another room while she and Hal had been eating pasta. As she drifted off she imagined Hal taking a bat to the back of Sam's head. Thank God they had made it out alive. The comfort of knowing they were Ok and probably the effects of the painkillers, let her sleep soundly. When she woke it was dark in her room. She could barely make out Sam sleeping in the corner chair.

"Wonder what time it is," she thought. Part of hospital mind tricks, no clocks or calendars. She evaluated her recovering body. Everything seemed warm and pain free for now. She hoped she wouldn't have to pee with her guest present. She was about to shift and close her eyes again when she heard Sam stir in the corner, he was standing. She didn't want him to go.

"Do you have to go?" She asked quietly, he moved closer. He put his hand on her forearm and she tried to turn to him. He pressed harder.

"Sam, you're on my arm." She was slightly annoyed, he was pinching the IV in her wrist.

She glanced up, it took her a fraction of a second to realize it wasn't Sam.

"Sam," hissed a familiar voice. "I should have killed him when I had the chance." Hal grabbed her other wrist pinning her to the bed, his face an inch away from hers. "I actually thought I had, no thanks to you." Hal grinned, his hair falling on her face.

She was too shocked to react. Oddly, she wasn't really afraid of him. Maybe because she had foiled his last attempt at killing her. Maybe because she couldn't really fathom this was real.

"Hal, please, I'm injured. My hands are burned." Maybe she could appeal to any feelings he might still have for her. He did let up, his face softened a bit.

Where were the nurses when you needed them? They were constantly bothering you while you slept or when you had visitors. Maybe this was one of her dreams. Where was Sam? Wasn't there a nurse call button somewhere? Her cell phone was on the nightstand.

He paused for a moment, looking at her with what seemed like regret. His silence began to unnerve her. She was slowly and carefully searching beside her in the bedding for the remote that would summon help. She searched her brain, was there anything sharp or heavy in the room?

"Hmm," he shook his head. "I didn't think this would be so difficult." He took something from his pocket and studied it, a syringe. He had drugged Sam, now he was going to drug her.

The fear began to rise, she frantically searched for the call button. She twisted awkwardly, sending a sharp pain down her leg. There was a twinge in her hand, the IV was slipping loose.

Hal took a deep breath, "The only thing that makes it better is that you won't feel much, it will be quick." She was trapped, she couldn't get out of bed, she couldn't run, how did it come to this? She moved as far away from him that the hospital bed would allow.

"Hal, they're going to know you did this, what can you possibly gain?" She felt the IV give way as she pulled back.

"Ha ha ha ha, really Bev, you're a smart girl, this is pure revenge, cleaning up loose ends." He grabbed the IV tube hanging above the IV bag. He wasn't going to inject her, he was going to put it in the IV, he didn't know she wasn't still connected. She had a chance. She turned her hand, pinching the tubing just above the IV needle that was now free from her hand.

"But Hal," she feigned panic, it wasn't hard, didn't her EKG register somewhere in this place, she was sure her heart rate was through the roof. He expertly injected the fluid into the tubing, the action was as chilling as the look on his face. Gone was the quirky crane-like countenance that endeared him to her. He was calculated, sharp as a blade, definitely lethal. She was no actress and she had no idea the symptoms the drugs were supposed to induce but she was going put on the best act of her life. After all, her life depended on it.

"No, Hal! No!" She tried to reach him, pretended to tear at the IV in her hand, she began breathing hard, "No! Help! Nurse!" She was screaming, he grabbed a pillow coming at her to silence her, she grabbed her chest, her breathing became shallow gasps. Hal could still actually smother her, she turned her head as he cover her face. She struggled.

"I'm sorry it didn't work out Bev." His face was right on top of hers, she struggled a bit more, the pillow muffling her screams, slowly she stopped moving. Did he believe her?

She shuddered and went limp, trying to calm her heart. She lay still, holding her breath for what seemed like eternity, her lungs were burning, much longer and she would pass out. She would have to come out swinging if she couldn't convince him she was dead.

"I'm sorry," he finally said again, slowly taking the pressure off of her.

She took a slow deep silent breath and held it again. As he lifted the pillow she gripped the IV needle and tubing in her hand. With one swift movement, she thrust the needle into his neck, at the same time she sat up and squeezed the drip bag. He never saw it coming. The needle and its deadly contents were at work before he could figure out that Bev wasn't dead and where he had been hit. He raised up, stumbling backward, clawing at his neck, shock crossed his face, then horror. He went down to his knees, finally pulling the deadly tubing from his neck and fell forward. He didn't move again.

"Nurse!" She screamed throwing herself into a coughing fit. Bev had seen enough horror and mystery movies to know that the killer was really never dead until help arrived. She found the damn button and pushed it over and over as she reached for her cell phone. She could hear footsteps running down the hall as she called 911, she watched Hal the whole time, just waiting for him to leap back up at her. Her whole body began to shake. Adrenaline, she had felt it too many times these past weeks.

Two nurses literally skidded into her room. Coming to a halt at the scene before them. Pausing for a moment in disbelief.

"Good God!" The first nurse crossed herself and scurried into action turning on lights. The second came to Bev's bedside and began taking inventory of equipment and patient. Help at last.

Before long Bev was in the middle of another emergency gathering of health and law enforcement professionals. Crime scene investigators came and took statements as well as the lethal medical equipment and the dead Hal Preston away. She had been in touch with Sam and Mac, they were on their way. Morning had come and noon was gone before her room was her own again. The adrenaline rush finally over, Bev's eyelids succumbed to exhaustion.

30

Clint sat patiently in the parlor of the doctor's home. He had been told Netty was resting. She had hit her head during the blast and broken her wrist. She was suffering from smoke inhalation and the coughing was draining her strength. The doctor would let him know shortly if she could have a visitor.

Clint felt wretched. Like a school boy waiting his turn with the school master. His stomach turned in anxious fits. He took a deep breath. He could smell the dried sweat on his smoky clothes, he hadn't even taken the time to clean up before coming. It didn't matter, all that mattered was that she was alive, that she would make it and maybe she would forgive him. In his wildest dreams she would not only forgive him but embrace him and let him make up for his mistakes by allowing him to care for her for the rest of their lives.

The nurse came from the hall.

"The Doctor said you can stay for a moment but you are not to tire her." She led the way down the hall to a small cool room in the back of the house.

The window shades were drawn, the light was dim, just a table lamp glowing at the bedside. Netty lay small and straight on the narrow bed. Her broken arm wrapped and slightly elevated at her side. He stood in the door frame, afraid to interrupt her rest, afraid to stir the perfect picture of her sleeping like a fair maiden. The nurse prodded him forward.

Hat in hand he moved beside the bed. She was so beautiful. Her blonde hair encircled her head like a halo, her skin was smooth. Hardly any indication that she had nearly perished hours ago.

She took a staggering breath and began to cough. Every exhalation wracking her small frame. The nurse helped her sit up partially, letting her gently back when the fit was over. Only then did she barely open her eyes.

She focused on Clint, recognizing him, he was sure. She turned her head and put her hand to her mouth.

"Miss Netty," he barely whispered. She did not respond. "Miss Netty," he paused, "I'm so sorry....Jacob is gone." She turned further from him. "The Belle is also gone." He waited, when she didn't respond, he decided to continue, "You, however, will be fine...you're alive and I am so thankful."

He walked to the end of the room, ran his hand through his disheveled hair and turned to her at the foot of the bed.

"I'm thankful because," his voice cracked, "I still love you, I love you more than anything in this world." He took a deep breath. "Now, I can only throw myself at your mercy with what I have left to say." The silence was only broken by her purposed breathing and the pounding of his heart in his ears.

"I started the fire," Clint blurted it out, like it tasted bad on his tongue. He could see the confusion on her brow even from this angle. "I heard who I thought was you and Jacob.....I couldn't stand the thought..." He wanted to cry, but he was too wrung out for any more tears. He turned his back to her instead, holding his hat in both hands.

He could barely push the air through his throat to say the rest.

"I threw a lit torch into the downstairs bedroom," an audible groan left his lips and the rest of the confession came tumbling out. "It must have hit a gas lamp. I killed my brother, whoever he was with and I burned the hotel down. It was all my fault."

He had nothing left. His shoulders fell, his knees felt weak, he reached for a small wooden chair and sat down. Netty didn't move.

"I'm so sorry." Clint rubbed his hands over his face, praying silently.

Time passed, too much time. An odd hollowness was sucking all the sound out of the room. He began to understand that his greatest fear, not his ardent dream, was coming true. Netty hated him, it was clear. He stood slowly, waited one moment more, but Netty still wouldn't react.

Nodding as if he understood her silence perfectly, he forced his usually sure feet to move and walked quietly out the door. His large hands trembled, and his faithful heart broke as he left to turn himself into the Sheriff.

Netty slowly rolled to her back, her eyes had an eerie light in them and a smile crept across her face.

"Take it and go, Netty, take it and go," she whispered to herself. Jace would proudly applaud the final curtain.

31

———

The air was crisp, the sky so clear that the color played tricks on the eyes. The high desert plateau had never looked more beautiful to Bev. The grass waved gracefully in a warm, easy, early summer breeze, its aroma intoxicating. She fairly flew over the ground, her dress was spinning and blowing around her ankles, she laughed, nothing hurt, no worries, nothing weighing her down.

On the near horizon stood a figure she recognized in an instant. Tall and handsome, eyes delighted to see her, he reached for her as she came to him. The comfort as he wrapped her in his arms was like no other man in her life, she breathed deeply. Nothing needed to be said, everything was understood, all was well between them.

Their embrace was interrupted. A police cruiser drove up over the edge of the field, showing off, fishtailing with tires spinning and dust flying. Her heart jumped. In the seat of that car was a big barreled officer in a brushed Stetson hat. She could see him grinning as he pulled up.

She went to him laughing, pausing only for a moment to look back at her father. But when she turned to him, he had already gone. For a fleeting moment she was sad, but not burdened with his departure like in times past. She turned back to the policeman, his grey eyes twinkling. He grabbed her up, spinning her around. She had never been so happy.

The sun raced across the plain in front of them and rested with a pink glow on the distant mountains. Its color got brighter and brighter and warmer and warmer until Bev had to put her forearm over her eyes. Everything was beginning to wash out, she reached for the man that had been beside her but he was gone. She was blinded by the intense light, blinking with no relief.

Bev sat up with a start. A dream. The evening sun was shining in her hospital room window, she shut her eyes again tight.

"Mmm," she moaned a bit, the hip was sore. She struggled to sit up to summon the nurse. She must have slept. She was in a mental fog.

"You all right?" A deep familiar voice came from across the room. She squinted, up on one elbow.

"Yes, fine thanks. Did I sleep a long time?" She stretched her shoulders and back.

"Don't know, want me to close the blinds?" He was up and moving before she answered.

"Thanks," when she was certain she could see him she looked up. Her confusion must have registered immediately. "Ethan?"

He chuckled, "Guess you were expecting someone else?" He sat down on the edge of the bed.

"But, why are you here?" She couldn't understand what would have possibly brought him. "How would he have known?" She thought. He was the last person she ever expected.

"You're kidding right? You almost died, twice!" He shrugged. "I'm still officially your next of kin." He started to reach for her but stopped himself, unsure.

"Wow. I had no idea...I'm sorry..." she didn't really know what to say. She hadn't thought of Ethan at all through any of her entire ordeal.

"No need to apologize." He stood up, easing the awkwardness between them. "I just wanted to be sure you were all right." He walked across the room. She knew him well enough to know that he had something else to say. She waited.

He turned back to her, genuine regret and caring on his face.

"It's just..." he checked his emotions, cleared his throat, "I was really worried, the thought of losing you permanently really shook me." He smiled carefully.

"Oh." She still was processing, what else could she say? "Thank you." She hung her head, a torrent of emotions were running through her mind.

"So, you'll be all right, right?" He inquired again.

"Yes! Of course! You know me, never down for long!" Her over exuberance was obvious to them both, so she rattled on. "I was in a fire." She held up her hands and pulled back her hair as proof. "And then I was injured in an accident trying to escape the fire so they had to replace my hip. I'm going to be fine."

He looked relieved.

"I'm really glad." He came back to the edge of the bed. He touched her arm with the back of his hand. She stayed very still, not knowing what it meant. "I want you to think about something..." he cleared his throat again, "You don't have to answer me now."

A sense of dread began to rise in her heart. She looked at him cautiously.

"This whole thing," he waved his arm indicating the hospital room and her condition, "Has made me think, I mean the feelings..." he struggled to find the words, "I want you to consider the possibility that...um, that we made a mistake." He looked at her squarely in the face. "Maybe we gave up to soon."

She drew in a breath, he may as well have slapped her. But she couldn't deny that she had thought it herself, in the first months. Her heart sank, she put her head on her bendable knee.

"Why now?" She wondered.

"Ethan..." she was finally able to muster, trying not to sound too much like a scolding school teacher.

"No, no. Don't answer now." He stood up and smiled. "I want you to get better, think about things while you're recouping."

She was about to discourage the entire thought when Sam bounded into the door frame.

"Hello, Darlin'!" He blurted it out before he realized she wasn't alone.

"Oh...hey!" He drew up quickly, containing himself.

There was a questioning silence for a moment as the men gave each other space.

"Um....Sam Gant....this is Ethan Connors. Ethan, this is Officer Sam Gant...he's the reason I'm here, not *here*, but still alive...." she smiled weakly at the two men.

She watched recognition pass across the cop's face.

"Ahhh, Mister Connors. Nice to meet you." Sam's body language said just the opposite.

"Same," said Ethan as they bridged the gap between them with a hand shake. There was more silence. Bev almost laughed at the irony of the situation before her, but managed to contain herself. It was all too real to be funny.

"Well then, thank you officer," Ethan finally offered. "She means a lot to me." He gathered his things.

"I'm going to take off, think about what I said Bev...let me know." He bent down and kissed her forehead. "I'm glad you're all right," he whispered. Bev looked beyond him at the stoic officer in the background.

"Thank you for coming all this way." She wanted to sound indifferent, but she didn't. Ethan left.

They both watched the doorway, waiting for Ethan to return or someone else to interrupt. No one came. Once again there was an abrupt and invisible wall separating them. Sam tried to act unconcerned.

"Soooo? Ethan?" He finally asked. Keeping his distance.

"Yes, Ethan. I had no idea he had been contacted." She wanted to reassure him, but didn't have the emotional energy. She leaned back on the raised bed, looking at the ceiling, trying to evaluate what just happened and what it meant to her.

Sam tried to lighten the mood.

"Hey! I came to tell you that you won't be charged for murder." He knew that it wasn't what was concerning her, but it was worth a try.

Bev smiled vaguely, "Oh! Yeah? I had almost forgotten that was a possibility."

He tried again, "What do they say about the hip? No further damage during the struggle?"

Bev didn't answer for a moment.

"I'm sorry, what did you say?" She finally responded.

"How are you feeling?" The question was loaded, he didn't mean physically.

She didn't look at him and took another moment to answer.

"I think I'm Ok, Sam." She finally met his gaze, looking at him seriously. "Ethan asked me to reconsider our divorce." She couldn't bear to see what emotion that might evoke from Sam, so she looked out the window.

"Wow," his response was flat.

"Yeah. Wow," she offered.

"Are you...I mean will you ....reconsider, I mean?" She could tell he wasn't sure he wanted to know the answer.

She took a deep breath, "I don't know." She wished she had a better response for him, but that was the best she could do for now. It was true, she didn't know.

Sam nodded and walked to the window, trying to see what she was seeing, maybe trying to help her find the answer.

They watched the sun set from two different places in the room, neither one spoke, it cast a pink glow on the mountains in the distance, then purple, then blue. They watched from two very different places in their hearts as well, feeling the palpable sadness for two different reasons. Bev from the inability to give her heart away and Sam because his heart was held captive, neither knowing how to overcome the other.

Sam turned when the sun disappeared. Bev looked into his grey eyes. She had seen those eyes shine with so many feelings, now she couldn't read the emotion there.

"You have a lot to think about." He turned to leave but suddenly changed his mind. He came back to the bed, Sam leaned down and kissed her tenderly. She kept her eyes closed letting the tears slide down her cheeks. She opened them to watch him walk away one more time.

The room was cold and pale. Bev was suddenly acutely aware that her whole body ached, her hip, her hands, her head and most of all...her heart.

EPILOGUE

After the fire had settled the town had a chance to sift through the ashes, attend to the wounded and assess the damages.

Many people had suffered, but none so much as Miss Netty Bingham. Public support for the refined young woman grew, just as public opinion of Mr. Clint Murray fell.

On the 15th of September of the year 1888, the Murrayville Gazette broke the news of their fate...

1 Cent

MURRAYVILLE GAZETTE

September 15, 1888   *   *   *   *   *   *   *   *   Volume 4, 19th Edition

Miss Netty Bingham, fiance of the late Mr. Jacob Murray, will continue renovations of the Belle hotel after last month's fire and near destruction of the building.

"I am fully recovered from my terrible ordeal in the fire and although my heart is still broken for the loss of my husband to be, the best way to honor his memory will be to continue on with our dream." Quotes Miss Bingham. The hotel construction will take 18 months to a year.

☞ AUCTION:

MURRAY RANCH

Miss Netty Bingham, betrothed of the late Mr. Jacob Murray, has announced the sale of the Murray ranch land and cattle company. All properties, assets and structures will be up for auction on:

SEPTEMBER 23

Auction will be held on site at the Murray ranch house. All sales final. All proceeds to secure the debts and finances of Miss Bingham.

* * * * *

PUBLIC HANGING

There will be a public hanging of three of the county's most notorious convicted criminals on Saturday at 10:00 in the town square.

Judd Hanson for robbery and murder of Samuel Carouth.

Clint Murray for arson and murder of Jacob Murray and Janine Simon.

Randall Oran for robbery and murder of Carl Hannigan.

Services will follow at Murrayville Baptist Church.

The End

For more titles by Robin Balogh Cox and
other great stories go to
knowheremedia.com/books

www.ingramcontent.com/pod-product-compliance
Lightning Source LLC
Chambersburg PA
CBHW070944180726
48291CB00004B/1126